A Flair for Goblins

A Flair for Goblins

A Sadie Kramer Flair Mystery

DEBORAH GARNER

CRANBERRY COVE PRESS

A Flair for Goblins
by Deborah Garner

First Printing – October 2020
ISBN: 9781952140051

Printed in the U.S.A

For all those who love mystery, ghosts, and goblins — or any combination of the above.

Books by Deborah Garner

The Paige MacKenzie Mystery Series

Above the Bridge
The Moonglow Café
Three Silver Doves
Hutchins Creek Cache
Crazy Fox Ranch

The Moonglow Christmas Novella Series

Mistletoe at Moonglow
Silver Bells at Moonglow
Gingerbread at Moonglow
Nutcracker Sweets at Moonglow
Snowfall at Moonglow
Yuletide at Moonglow

The Sadie Kramer Flair Series

A Flair for Chardonnay
A Flair for Drama
A Flair for Beignets
A Flair for Truffles
A Flair for Flip-Flops
A Flair for Goblins

Cranberry Bluff

ONE

Sadie Kramer dropped two slices of wheat bread into the toaster and stood before her refrigerator, looking at the calendar that hung by two clips shaped like vegetables. Although the whimsical magnets were intended to remind her to eat healthy, her kitchen's contents rarely met the goal. Pasta, yes. Scones, usually. Chocolate, absolutely.

Renewing her daily vow to shop more carefully, Sadie poured a cup of coffee, grabbed the toast when it popped up, and took a seat at the kitchen table. "One more week until the Wainwright Spooktacular, Coco." She took a sip of the hot beverage and looked at the petite Yorkie as if expecting a comment in return. "We need to be at the mansion by two this afternoon." Coco tilted her head to the side and eyed Sadie's toast enviously. "I'm not sure how I got corralled into helping, but it is what it is. I'm not about to go back on a promise."

Not that she had much of a choice. Seymour Wainwright's wife, Roberta, had been a longtime customer of Flair, Sadie's San Francisco fashion boutique. The offer to assist with the Halloween event slipped out of her mouth accidentally while Roberta was deciding between a conservative navy pantsuit and an aquamarine silk dress with a wilder vibe to it. Somehow, in the course of selling the apparel, she'd also sold her right to a quiet last week of October.

The Seymour Wainwright Foundation was a high-profile

organization, much more so than many of the smaller charities around. As such, helping with the fund-raising event not only served to aid the local community, it furthered the business interests of Flair. Word of mouth was always the best method of advertising, and that couldn't be done well without stepping out and letting people know the boutique existed. Sure, she had many regular customers, but there were always new ones to find.

"It'll be fine, Coco," Sadie said as she finished her coffee. She tossed the Yorkie a morsel of toast, which Coco deftly caught midair and consumed. She placed both her mug and plate in the sink. "Amber will run the store, doing an excellent job as always. And you and I will brave the legendary spirits of the Wainwright mansion."

She'd never believed in ghosts or superstition of any sort, not even as a young girl, which was more decades ago than she cared to count. Stepping on cracks never seemed to bother her mother's back, walking under ladders only served to shorten the distance between point A and point B, and she'd always been fond of cats. Seeing one cross in front of her, black or otherwise, was a treat right down to the last swishy whisk of feline tail. Therefore, she paid no mind to the many rumors about the Wainwright mansion being haunted. She'd heard the tales for years, and they meant nothing to her.

Donning black slacks and a bright orange tunic—appropriate for the upcoming holiday—she settled Coco in her tote bag and headed to the boutique, where she found Amber, covered with artificial cobwebs, in the front display window.

"Decorating the window? Or decorating yourself?" She couldn't resist teasing the young assistant, who sported more cobwebs than either of the two mannequins in the display.

"I'm not sure at this point," Amber admitted. She brushed a few strands of stretchy gray fiber off her arms and climbed down from the window. "I just thought sprucing things up a bit would be entertaining for customers."

"An excellent idea," Sadie said as she placed Coco on a velvet pillow that served as the Yorkie's regular seating area on the countertop. The plush location allowed Coco to observe those coming and going, as well as to receive more than her fair share of attention.

Amber circled behind the sales counter, gave Coco a pat on the head, and then picked up a note. "Oh, Roberta Wainwright called about twenty minutes ago and wanted you to call her back. She sounded pretty rattled. I think it's about the Spooktacular event."

Sadie nodded. "Yes. I told her I'd help with it. I'm headed over there this afternoon."

"What kind of help?" Amber asked.

"I don't know, to be honest," Sadie said. "Decorations maybe? Setting up a refreshment area? Odds and ends?" She shrugged her shoulders. "It doesn't matter. It's for a good cause."

"You're not worried?" Amber placed her hands on her hips and frowned.

"Worried? About what?"

"The superstitions? That place is supposed to be haunted," Amber said. "*Really* haunted. When we were kids, we'd dare each other to walk up the front steps."

"And did you?"

"Sometimes," Amber said. "But it made me nervous. Other times I'd find an excuse to leave. I'd say something like my mother needed me home early, or I had piano lessons or something. You really don't know the stories?"

Sadie polished a smudge on the counter with her tunic sleeve. "Oh, I probably heard them a long time ago, but I think all that stuff is nonsense, so there's no point in cluttering my memory with it."

"But maybe you should know what you're in for. I mean, that place is scary even from the outside. I've heard it's still scary after all the renovations and upgrades. When the other kids and I walked up the front steps, we'd *hear* things, though the mansion was supposed to be empty." Amber shuddered.

"What kinds of things?"

"Like someone wailing or the sound of breaking glass. One time we heard a loud bang or pop, and we all thought it might have been a gunshot." Amber's frown deepened. "Let me tell you at least one story, just so you'll be prepared, just in case you see or hear something."

"If it will make you feel better, of course I'll listen to a story." Sadie settled on a stool near the register.

"Well, you know the Wainwright family built that mansion in the 1800s, right?"

Sadie nodded.

"So it goes that tragedy after tragedy kept befalling the Wainwrights. The first owner's youngest son, Branton, shot his older sister, Tabitha, with a hunting rifle in the ballroom, and then he turned the gun on himself. No one knew why he did it. They were both dressed for a party that was supposed to go on that night to celebrate All Hallows' Eve. When their mother and the housekeeper found the bodies, both women screamed and screamed. The mother ran to the top floor of the mansion, still screaming, and threw herself out of a window. That may be why we kept hearing shattering glass. And the wailing.

"A friend of mine was part of a renovation crew years ago,

and he swears at one point when he was working on the wainscoting in the ballroom that he could see the walls sort of… how did he put it? Undulating? Like someone was *in* the walls, trying to get out."

Sadie stood and brushed invisible dust off her knees. "Well, that does sound disturbing. Your friend must have quite the imagination."

"Oh, he's not the only one with a story like that. A workman hired to replace the mansion's windows kept finding this one window on the top floor shattered. Every time he'd replace it, the next day when he returned to work, that window would be shattered. I don't know why that finally stopped happening, but it did."

"Weird," Sadie said. "I'll make sure to avoid broken glass."

"Well, I can tell you don't believe the stories are true, but thanks for listening. You're more practical about this kind of stuff than I am. It's one of the things I admire about you." Amber smiled at her boss. "I really don't like scary stuff."

"What about movies?" Sadie said as she checked her hair in a mirror near the front counter. She'd taken the color back to a basic gray shade recently and wondered if some of the cobweb fiber Amber was using for the window might add a touch of texture. "Like *The Exorcist* or *Poltergeist* or *Nightmare on Elm Street*?"

"No, no, and no." Amber shook her head. "I'm more of a Hallmark Channel girl. Oh, by the way…" She reached under the counter and brought out a small box. "Matteo sent these over."

Sadie's eyes lit up. "Something new?" Not that it mattered. Anything from Cioccolato, the gourmet chocolate shop her friend Matteo ran next door, would be divine. She opened the box and smiled. Ghosts, pumpkins, black bats, and witch hats graced the tops of square chocolate truffles.

"Cute, aren't they?" Amber set the box next to the register, far enough away from Coco to not be within easy access. "Matteo said to put them out as samples for customers. I just wanted to show you first."

"I think I should test one," Sadie offered. "You know, for quality control." Looking over the selection, she picked a white-chocolate truffle with a black bat on top. Popping it in her mouth, she closed her eyes and sighed. "He can do no wrong over there in that magical chocolate shop."

A jangle signaled the front door opening. Sadie and Amber both greeted the customer who entered, a middle-aged woman who returned the greeting and then began to browse selections.

"So, what are you dressing up as?" Amber asked, turning to Sadie. "For the Spooktacular?"

"Huh," Sadie said, momentarily puzzled. "I hadn't thought about it. I'm not even sure I'll be going. I offered to help Roberta set up, that's all."

"Well, she'll probably rope you into going. And you have to wear a costume if you do," Amber pointed out. "Everyone dresses up for that event."

"Then Coco will need a costume too," Sadie said. She pulled a string of faux cobweb from Amber's sweater and held it against her head as she looked in the mirror again. Unsure, she placed the string back on Amber's sweater and ate another truffle, this one dark chocolate with a ghost on top.

"You could be Dorothy from *The Wizard of Oz*, and Coco could be Toto," Amber suggested. "Not too original, I suppose."

"Maybe I'll just wear cat ears and dress in all black," Sadie suggested. "It would be easy, and I could arrange it at the last minute if I end up going."

"That sounds awfully basic for your personality," Amber said. "How about dressing as a witch?"

"Are you calling me a witch?" Sadie feigned displeasure.

"A *good* witch," Amber clarified. "Or you could be Wonder Woman. Or a nurse."

"And Coco?" Sadie said. "We don't have to match, you know."

"Maybe a cowgirl," Amber suggested. "You could put a cowboy hat on her and add a vest and western bandanna."

A new voice entered the conversation as the customer approached the counter to make a purchase. "My Chihuahua is going to be a taco," she said. "And I'm dressing up as a bottle of hot sauce. This will add a touch of whimsy." She waved a red silk scarf in the air and then deposited it on the counter.

"I see," Sadie replied, at a loss for any other response. Amber simply nodded.

"I have a straight red dress that goes to my ankles and a black hat that looks like a bottle top." The woman fished her wallet out of an oversized purse and handed Amber a credit card. After signing the charge slip, she replaced the card in her wallet and left with her newly purchased scarf.

Amber turned to Sadie again. "You see, anything goes. How about a ballet dancer?"

Sadie shook her head. "My ballet figure up and did a grand jeté out of here years ago, and Coco has a terrible fear of tutus."

"Oh, right," Amber said. "I remember that now."

"Yes," Sadie said. "Terrible incident. We mustn't talk about it in front of her." Coco, hearing the word *her*, lifted her head from the pillow and leveled a gaze at Sadie and Amber. "You see what I mean?" Sadie continued. "Taboo subject."

"My lips are sealed," Amber vowed. "I suppose I should get back to the window display while we're between customers."

Sadie nodded. "I'd like to get some work done on the account books before we go to the mansion. I promised Roberta I'd meet her at two." She glanced at her fitness wristband to check the time, finally having given in to the trend of tracking steps. "Looks like I have plenty of extra time. I'll be in the office."

Grabbing another truffle, Sadie headed for the back hallway. Coco trotted along right behind her, strangely imitating her walk.

Once seated at her desk, Sadie fired up her computer and ran a search for pet costumes as she nibbled on the truffle. She patted her lap, and Coco hopped up. "What about that one?" she said, pointing to an image of a beagle dressed as Gumby. Coco just blinked in response. "Or maybe this," she continued, indicating a corgi disguised as a pumpkin, green stem hat on its head. Coco blinked again and then closed her eyes. "I'll take that as a no," Sadie said. After several other attempts to interest Coco in a costume, she picked up the note Amber had taken.

Please call Roberta ASAP!!!

"Three exclamation marks? That seems a little dramatic, don't you think, Coco?" The Yorkie, now sound asleep on Sadie's lap, didn't respond. "I guess I'll call her back even though I'll be seeing her soon."

The phone rang only once before a woman's voice cried into the phone, "Hello? Hello?"

"Hi, Roberta? It's Sadie Kramer. You left a message with my store manager. She said it was important. I'll be there as promised to help you this afternoon, don't worry."

"Oh, Sadie! Thank you for getting back to me. Could you come at noon instead of two? Seymour had to go out of town to handle a snafu in a development deal in Houston, and I can't find the decorations he said he'd had delivered. The

Spooktacular is such fun to plan, but it always turns me into a veritable tub of nerves! I just need… help."

Sadie muffled a sigh and ran a finger over the top of Coco's soft head. So much for getting a bit of paperwork done before she left for the mansion.

"Of course I can be there at noon, Roberta. I'm happy to help in any way I can. Do you need me to pick up anything on the way there?" Sadie crossed her fingers, hoping the answer would be no. She didn't particularly want to be hauling cardboard skeletons or witches' brooms in her little car.

"No, no, I *know* everything is here somewhere. It's just vanished. Poof. Like smoke or fog or something. This mansion is so big, and I can't remember where Seymour said the delivery people were going to put the decorations. He's also not answering his cell phone, which isn't at all like him!"

Sadie wondered if that was exactly like him, but she'd only met Seymour a couple of times, once at a cocktail party when the foundation was raising funds for a sea lion rescue organization and another time when he came into Flair to purchase an outfit, though Amber had been the one to wait on him. So she really didn't know.

"I'll be there at noon, and I'll do whatever I can to help you set up everything. It will be fine. Remember, this is supposed to be fun!"

"Yes, yes, well, I do wonder if the house somehow, you know, gobbled up all those spiders and goblins and monsters." Roberta took a deep breath. "Thank you, Sadie. I feel calmer already."

Sadie ended the phone call, shut down the computer, and softly nudged Coco to wake her up. "We'll have to choose costumes later. If we even need them. For now, let's go find out exactly what help Roberta Wainwright needs."

TWO

The Wainwright mansion looked fairly innocent from the street, at least when Sadie pulled up to the curb. Hardly the haunted house it was rumored to be. The three-story Victorian structure sat back approximately fifty feet, flanked by a massive lawn dotted with hedges, flowers, and well-manicured trees. A wrought iron fence surrounded the property, which took up an entire city block. Only the No Trespassing signs and overcast sky—which clearly had nothing to do with the building itself—gave off a foreboding air.

"Nothing too scary about this place," Sadie said to Coco as she unbuckled the tiny harness that the Yorkie wore as a seat belt. "At least not from the outside." Talking to Coco was a common habit that helped Sadie clear her mind at times. She found it reassuring if not somewhat lopsided since the petite canine never disagreed with her. Not verbally, that is. Sadie did suspect a few of Coco's expressions implied uncertainty if not downright skepticism.

The only other car on the street aside from hers was a dilapidated economy car with a dent in one fender parked a couple of houses down. It was odd that Roberta's car was missing. Surely she would have driven there. The woman didn't seem the type to take public transportation, and she certainly wouldn't be caught dead in a car like the one parked down the street. She had a tendency to flaunt her wealth by driving upscale vehicles and wearing expensive jewelry. However, it was always possible the Mercedes she usually parked in front of Flair could be in the shop. A friend might have dropped her off. Or she could have taken a taxi.

Gathering Coco into her arms, she closed the car door and beeped the alarm to lock it. Giving Coco the six-foot stretch that her leash allowed, she wandered about while Coco sniffed the grass selectively and finally paused at a self-approved spot to take care of business.

Continuing their full-circle stroll around the mansion, Sadie estimated the size of the building to be at least eight thousand square feet, possibly nine thousand, taking all three floors into account. It appeared freshly painted, which made sense in view of its historical designation. Perhaps funding regulations—she remembered reading in a newspaper article that the foundation had received a grant—required a certain amount of upkeep. Not knowing the specifics required to keep a historical structure in shape, Sadie figured one ingredient was certain: money and plenty of it.

The Wainwright family was known to travel in upper social circles, having made their fortune in oil. It was public knowledge that there had been several disagreements between siblings about finances, which the media covered like sharks going after bait. Sadie couldn't remember the details, not being fond of gossip-oriented news based mostly on conjecture. But her friend Myrtle often called or sent texts with the juicy details. In families like this, trust funds were sometimes at the root of the disputes, as well as questionable changes in wills. According to the tabloids that Myrtle followed, Roberta Wainwright was wealthy on her own, heiress to a man who built his fortune on hair care products or skin-care products.

Sadie wasn't sure. What she did know was that Roberta had never been broke, and it showed in her behavior.

Calling Coco over to her, Sadie placed her in the tote that served as Coco's travel compartment when out on excursions or visiting places that weren't specifically pet friendly. She folded the Yorkie's leash—a stylish, sparkly pumpkin print that suited the season—and placed it inside the bag.

All set for whatever tasks Roberta had arranged for her, Sadie circled around the building and climbed up a number of marble steps to the front door. Unsure whether to ring one of several buttons that looked like doorbells, tap with her knuckles to announce her presence, or simply step inside, she decided using the hefty iron door knocker would be most appropriate. Surely it was what someone would have done back in the late 1800s when the mansion was built.

Sadie wrapped her hand around the lion's-head ball attached to the door, surprised momentarily by the sensation of cold metal against her palm. She tapped the knocker lightly at first and waited for a response, but there was nothing, not even the sound of footsteps approaching from within. She knocked again, this time more boldly, but there was still no answer. Trying one last time, she whacked away with more force than she deemed necessary. Expecting to finally be greeted, she was surprised when the door swung open a few inches, a creaking sound from the hinges accompanying the movement.

"Odd," she muttered, pushing the door open farther but remaining outside. She stuck her head in the doorway and called out. "Roberta?" There was no answer. She stepped inside the entryway and called out again. "Roberta, are you there?" Still nothing.

A sudden gust of wind chose that moment to blow the door

behind her shut. She jumped, and Coco scrambled to the top of the tote, wide-eyed. "It's fine," she whispered in an attempt to calm both herself and the Yorkie. "We can't get carried away by silly rumors now, can we?" She eased Coco back into the bag and stroked her fur. "Houses aren't haunted, including this one. We just need to find Roberta and see what she needs."

Sadie crossed the marbled tiles, listening to her footsteps echo. Looking up, she estimated the ceiling, framed by a circular stairway that accessed all three floors, to be a good thirty feet high. The walls were as slick as the flooring, with only a gilded framed painting here and there to break up the expanse. Without carpet or furnishings in the foyer, there was nothing to absorb the sound. Surely it would echo. She could only imagine how muddled conversations would be with a crowd in the space where she stood.

Stepping into the closest room, she was delighted to see a large throw rug surrounded by a variety of antiques appropriate for the original period of the mansion. Undoubtedly, some were replicas, but others—an emerald-green velvet Chesterfield lounge, a tufted corner chaise in an ecru tone, and a tall mahogany sideboard—appeared to be authentic at first glance. Yet she found it inconceivable that a rosewood triple-filigree settee she spotted below arched windows at the front of the room could be original. She'd seen one just like it at a museum in Boston. The extravagant piece was valued close to forty thousand dollars. Certainly a mansion open to the public wouldn't have such a piece out in the open, not for an event where a child—or tipsy adult—might accidentally sit on spilled candy corn.

She moved to the opposite side of the foyer and attempted to open a carved set of double doors but found them locked.

"Come on, Coco," Sadie said, directing her voice to the

opening of her tote. "Let's find Roberta. I'm sure she's here somewhere. She must be." Even as she said the words, a chill began to set in. She shivered but then calmed down. It wasn't outside the realm of reason that someone in a house that large might not hear a person enter. Yet, even considering the multiple floors, the echo seemed loud enough to carry her voice throughout the building.

A continued search of the ground floor proved fruitless. Not only was Roberta nowhere to be found, but there was no one on the floor at all. That didn't surprise Sadie. It was only logical that anyone there would have acknowledged her presence. But if no one was there, why was the front door ajar?

Sadie ran through a variety of possibilities. Roberta could be listening to music through headphones that prevented her from hearing Sadie's arrival. Or perhaps a housekeeper with a hearing impairment was on an upper floor, cleaning. Said person might have neglected to close the front door all the way. Or the walls might simply be too thick for sound to travel, even with the echoes factored in. Still, Roberta had been so frantic when they spoke that Sadie was surprised she wasn't waiting in the foyer for her arrival.

Sadie hushed the misgivings she'd started to feel and took several steps up the winding staircase that led from the foyer to the second floor. Each step seemed to creak more than the one before it, which did nothing to calm Sadie's growing nerves. Even Coco peeked out of the tote and looked down at the steps as if expecting them to rattle or perhaps even bark.

If she counted correctly, she'd climbed twenty-two steps by the time she reached the second-floor landing. An intricately carved owl's head at the top of the banister signaled her arrival. She called out Roberta's name again, and again she heard no response. Tiptoeing down the hallway that ran off the landing, she moved from one room to another, checking inside each. She found additional settees, armoires, claw-foot tables, and sleigh beds, but no sign of another human being. Not a maid with a hearing problem. Not a caretaker wearing earbuds. Not Roberta.

She finished her rounds of the second floor and looked up the stairway to the third. By this time, Coco was becoming restless, shuffling around in the tote. Sadie knew that animals could often sense things before humans could, and this did nothing to calm her nerves. Taking Coco's behavior into account, she debated returning to the first floor instead of searching the upper floor. It would be easy enough to call Roberta later to see if something had come up that meant she had to leave the mansion before noon. Still, she had already covered the second floor, with only one floor left to explore. She might as well take a quick look.

She'd only taken a few steps up the stairs when a dull thud echoed from below. Coco's head popped up, and Sadie paused and listened but heard nothing else. "Roberta?" she called down the stairs. Again, nothing. As she took another couple of steps, she heard the sound of breaking glass. *The breaking glass that Amber mentioned?* Clasping the banister tightly with one hand, she held the other hand to her chest to catch her breath while her tote bag swung from the crook of her arm. *What to do? What to do?* The thought of leaving the mansion immediately was appealing, but it also seemed irresponsible. What if someone was injured and needed her help?

"Is anyone there? Is everything all right?" Sadie called out again, receiving only silence in return.

She couldn't leave without finding out more. There were plenty of possible causes for the sound below. A window might have blown open, slamming with a thud against the wall, and the wind might have knocked a glass vase to the floor, its fragments crashing on the hardwood or marble. Or maybe the window slammed shut again and its panes shattered. Yes, Sadie told herself. Certainly it was one of those possibilities.

"I say we quickly check the rooms up above, Coco," Sadie said as she continued to the third floor. She hugged the tote bag, wiggling Yorkie and all, against her chest. "Then we'll make sure everything downstairs is all right. We'll secure the window or whatever made the sound and then leave."

Feeling reassured, Sadie turned her attention back to the third floor. She took a deep breath and then exhaled slowly, willing any misgivings to flow out with the air from her lungs. She found herself in a long hallway, half leading to her right, the other half to her left. She flipped a mental coin and headed to the right.

Knowing the mansion contained nine bedrooms and seven bathrooms, she was not at all surprised to find most rooms held antique beds, dressers, and a variety of rugs, lamps, and general articles of room decor. Paintings hung on most walls, whether oil or acrylic she couldn't tell. The artwork ranged from peaceful pastoral scenes to family portraits, some stern to the point of discomfort. At least they felt uncomfortable to view and likely had felt the same for the person who'd posed. Small brass plaques rested below each painting, but Sadie continued from one room to the next without stopping to read them.

After she confirmed that nothing seemed amiss in the right hallway, Sadie retraced her steps to the stairway and searched the rooms to the left. Again, she found bedrooms, several washrooms, and a utility closet that stored cleaning supplies for the housekeeping staff who maintained the premises. A recessed alcove toward the end of the hallway offered a view to the front of the property. Sadie paused briefly, comforted by the tranquil state of the grounds.

Certain that she'd overreacted to the earlier sound, she returned to the third-floor landing and began her descent. "We'll just finish up, Coco, and then head home," she said as she continued downstairs. "I feel certain all is well."

And that's exactly how she did feel until she returned to the foyer and noticed the doors to the locked room were now ajar. Taking a quick peek inside, she gasped. There, in the middle of the ballroom, the body of a woman lay splayed upon an exquisitely polished wood floor. An elaborate chandelier rested against the woman's head as if she'd chosen to wear it as a hat. Dozens of crystal pieces dotted the surrounding floor while others still clung to the lighting fixture itself.

Equally terrified and intrigued, Sadie took a few steps into the room, just enough to try to get a closer look at the face. Oddly, it was covered with a mask and therefore not identifiable. However, the necklace dangling from the person's neck was all Sadie needed to see. She'd sold that piece of jewelry herself at Flair. To the regular customer who now lay surrounded by glass, metal, and a touch of blood. A customer who would no longer be doing any shopping: Roberta Wainwright.

THREE

"When exactly did you enter the building?"

Sadie sat on the front steps of the mansion, staring into the street. The shock of discovering Roberta's body was still too fresh to think clearly. She'd been around death before, at least in the general vicinity. She'd even helped solve a few murder cases. But she'd never actually *found* the victim. There'd always been one or two degrees of separation. Either she'd arrived at a scene after it was roped off, or she'd been informed of the person's demise. Once she'd had the misfortune to witness a death in a café, but she'd been with other people, not alone. In addition, the deceased had never been someone who she'd planned to meet up with. It had always been a wrong place, wrong time sort of thing. This situation was all new territory.

"I'm... I'm sorry," Sadie said, realizing someone was speaking to her. She turned toward the voice, finding a middle-aged man with a badge hanging on a lanyard around his neck. A detective, and not just any detective. She'd recognize that receding hairline and expanding waistline anywhere, though the faint hint of a mustache was new. *Froggy!*

"Detective." Sadie attempted a friendly smile. "A pleasure to see you."

"Likewise," the detective said, not sounding at all sincere. "And what a surprise to see you at... let's see... oh, a murder scene!"

"I can only imagine," Sadie said dryly. "What was the question again?"

"What time did you enter the Wainwright mansion?"

Sadie considered the question and answered with another. "What time is it now?"

The detective flicked his wrist to check his watch. "Twelve forty-seven."

"Twelve o'clock," Sadie said.

"No, twelve forty-seven," the detective repeated.

"You asked what time I entered the mansion," Sadie said.

"That's correct."

"Twelve o'clock." Sadie looked at the detective as if seeing him for the first time. Perhaps the initial shock was wearing off. She felt a sudden need to focus. She leaned forward to read the name on his badge just to be sure she hadn't lost her mind. *Detective Frogert.* "I arrived here at twelve o'clock. Noon. So that's when I entered." She watched as the detective jotted down notes on a pad he'd pulled from his pocket. "Wait, that's not correct," she said.

"You didn't enter the building at twelve o'clock?"

"No," Sadie clarified. "I arrived at the property then, but I walked around the grounds before going to the front door."

"About how long would you say?"

Sadie looked at the nearest hedges as if they might give her an answer. "About five minutes."

The detective tapped his pen in a triple motion against his mustache, which Sadie found annoying for some reason. She was beginning to remember how Froggy raised the snark in her. "Detective Frogert, you've grown yourself a mustache!"

Froggy ran a finger across the fur on his upper lip. "Yes. The wife wanted to see what I'd look like with a mustache. I did it for her."

"Of course you did. You look dashing." Not that Sadie believed her own words. She thought the mustache made his face look even broader.

"So, why did you decide to do that?"

"To do what?" Sadie wondered whether she hadn't heard the question or if the mustache-tapping was distracting her.

"To walk around the property," the detective said. "What made you decide to do that?"

"I didn't see any reason not to," Sadie said. "The landscaping is lovely, and Roberta's car wasn't here yet. I thought I might be early." She thought that over as soon as the words left her mouth. She could have sworn Roberta was already at the mansion when she and Sadie talked just before Sadie left Flair.

Detective Frogert looked up and down the street and then turned back to Sadie. "You say the victim's car wasn't here?"

"That's correct," Sadie said. "Only an old car down the block."

"What old car?" Detective Frogert looked out again.

Sadie peered down the street and frowned. "I don't see it now, but there was definitely a car there when I arrived."

"Can you describe it?"

"Not really," Sadie said. "Some kind of small car. I remember it had a dent in one fender."

"Color?"

"I didn't notice." Sadie tried to recall anything specific about the vehicle, but only the dent came to mind. "Something basic, I guess. Nothing flashy or I would remember. In any case, it wasn't anyone here. The mansion was empty."

"Perhaps it belonged to someone who was just leaving," the detective suggested.

"I didn't see anyone," Sadie said. That was accurate, but the detective had a point. Someone could have left out a back entrance at the same time she arrived at the front. The possibility made her wish she'd lingered outside longer. Perhaps she would have seen someone leave. Then again, the person might have been watching her while waiting to leave. A shiver ran up her spine.

Sadie watched a coroner's vehicle pull up along with another police car. Two officers entered the building, one with a camera, the other with what Sadie took to be a fingerprint kit. At least it resembled those she'd seen on *Law and Order*.

"Did your friend have any enemies that you know of? Family disputes? Anything like that?" Detective Frogert held his pen over the notepad.

"She wasn't my friend," Sadie said. No sooner had the words left her mouth, she felt a need to clarify but didn't get the chance.

"I see," the detective said, eyebrows raised. "An enemy, perhaps?"

"Of course not." Sadie bristled. "She was just a regular customer at my shop, Flair. Perhaps you remember it? The fashion boutique next door to Cioccolato, the gourmet chocolate shop?"

Detective Frogert remained silent and scratched his head with his pen, which Sadie found strange enough that she wished he would switch back to the triple mustache tap. "Yes, unfortunately, I remember it well. It's interesting how your customers seem to be in the habit of getting themselves murdered. So how did you end up here?" he asked.

"I offered to help with the Spooktacular charity fundraiser because Roberta said she was shorthanded," Sadie said. "Besides, it was a good excuse to see the Wainwright mansion. I've never been inside before and wondered if it would live up to all those articles about it in architectural magazines."

Another car pulled up to the curb, this one screeching into place, narrowly missing the back of the coroner's vehicle. A man in his thirties jumped out, slammed the car door, and bolted up the walkway. An officer stopped him at the front door, and a heated interaction followed. Both Sadie and the detective watched as the man pulled out his wallet. After handing over what Sadie assumed to be identification, he was allowed to enter.

"Now that's a car I would remember," Sadie said, pointing to the shiny copper Jaguar the man had left at the curb. "It's definitely not the old one that was parked down the street earlier."

"Excuse me a moment, Ms. Kramer," Detective Frogert said. He turned toward the building and walked up to the front door. Sadie tried unsuccessfully to hear the conversation between the detective and the officer, but she was certain it involved the man who'd left his fancy vehicle moments before.

"Ah, Coco." Sadie sighed. She reached into the tote balanced on her lap and patted the Yorkie's head while looking up and down the street. A growing crowd of curious people had gathered in front, watching the police activity. "How do I get myself into these situations?" The double yip that followed sounded like a cross between a laugh and a reprimand. "Now, that's not really fair, Coco. I was doing a good deed. I wouldn't have been here at all if Roberta hadn't asked me to help her. Tricked me is more like it. She caught me off guard when I was helping her decide between those two outfits." Coco sneezed, a response Sadie couldn't quite interpret. "You're right, I should have said no. Maybe she would have purchased something anyway."

"Talking to someone?"

Sadie looked up to see that Detective Frogert had returned.

Growing weary of questions at this point, she debated telling him the ghost of the deceased was on the sidewalk and they were having a lively conversation. Instead, she gave him the true answer. "My bag," she said, indicating the tote on her lap. "I'm talking to my tote bag."

He peered inside the tote bag just long enough to see the tops of the Yorkie's ears. Coco let out a string of yips. "That dog!" He scooted away about a foot.

"Yes, Detective, I believe you two are acquainted."

"Glad to see it's in good health."

"*She's* in good health."

"Fine, fine, *she*. Well, I think that's all I need from you at the moment. You're free to go. Just don't…"

"I know. I know," Sadie said, finishing his sentence for him. "Don't leave town."

Detective Frogert frowned. "That's such a cliché, Ms. Kramer. Next you'll be offering me donuts. I was going to say don't end up at any more murder scenes. This seems to be a habit of yours." He pulled a card from his pocket and handed it to her. "Just in case you lost my card from last time. Call me if you think of anything else that might be helpful."

"Of course." She watched him walk up the stairs to the front of the mansion, and she pulled her keys out of the tote bag. But suddenly a wave of exhaustion mixed with shock came over her, and she lacked the energy to remain standing. She sat down to wait for her nerves to be steady enough for her to drive. Coco popped her head up out of the bag, and Sadie leaned down toward her. "I don't know what I'd do without you, Coco." The Yorkie licked her nose.

She sensed a presence nearby and looked up as the Jaguar driver sat down to her right. He sighed and put his face in his hands.

"Are you all right?" Sadie asked.

He raised his head and looked at her. "You're the one who found my mother's body?"

Sadie winced, now realizing who he was. "Yes. I'm so, so sorry."

"They wouldn't let me see her. They only allowed me in as far as the foyer. Can you tell me… anything at all? He clasped his hands together as if he were praying. She noticed they were shaking.

"I really don't think I can, not right now," Sadie said. She wasn't sure the police would want her telling anyone else what she'd seen before they'd examined the scene and body more thoroughly, not even Roberta's son. They would have already told him anything they wanted him to know. "I may be able to later, but I don't feel up to it right now. Again, I'm sorry." Sadie patted the young man's folded hands. "I'm Sadie Kramer. Your mother often shopped at my boutique, Flair. My assistant and I will miss her."

"Cooper Wainwright. Wayward child, oldest of two, and black sheep of the family. Or maybe the prodigal son. Mother and I'd had a falling out, but we were starting to grow close again."

"A falling out?"

"Yes. You know how these things go. Her generation is so stubborn, and she wouldn't listen to any of my suggestions. She treated me like a toddler even though I'm thirty-eight." He sighed. "Never mind. That was all behind us. I can't believe she's gone. This never would have happened if Dwight hadn't taken the day off."

"Dwight?"

"The caretaker," Cooper said. "He's been with us for decades, and he's very protective of the mansion. He never would have let a stranger in."

Sadie wanted badly to ask Cooper more about the disagreements with his mother, but she knew now was not the time.

He turned and looked directly at Sadie, his gray eyes dark with what Sadie guessed was grief. He was beautiful in a pale, fragile way, like Wedgewood china. "What were you doing here anyway?"

"Roberta… your mother… asked me to help her with preparations for the Spooktacular."

"Of course. That party stresses her every year, and Dad being out of town didn't help. I dropped her off this morning and planned to take her out to lunch to give her a break. But then this happened." Cooper waved his hand toward the mansion.

Froggy appeared again at the top of the steps. "Mr. Wainwright? If you don't mind, we have a few more questions for you. I'm sure Ms. Kramer would like to get on her way."

Cooper stood and reached down to help Sadie up. "Of course, Detective. I'll be right there."

"Wait just a minute," Sadie said. She dug through a side pocket of her tote until she found a small business card holder. She pulled out one of her Flair cards and handed it to Cooper. "If you need anything, anything at all, please feel free to call me. And again, I'm so sorry about your dear mother."

Cooper took the card and tucked it into his shirt pocket. "Thank you, Ms. Kramer. I may take you up on that offer."

Sadie watched Cooper join Froggy and a uniformed officer, then turned to start walking toward her car. When she reached the sidewalk, she paused, cradled the tote bag in her arms, and spoke directly to her dog. "Coco, we might have to have something a little more medicinal than chardonnay tonight. Maybe some chamomile tea with a splash of honey. Something calming. This has been terribly upsetting."

When she raised her head, she realized a young man was standing directly in front of her, and she'd nearly bumped into him. Her nerves already on edge from the events of the day, the man's sudden appearance gave her a start. "Oh, I'm so sorry! I didn't see you there!"

"No problem. I always seem to be getting in the way of someone. I'm Keith Cross."

"Sadie Kramer. I really should have been watching where I was going, but I've had a bit of a shock, you see."

Keith Cross was dressed much like Froggy, though his wrinkled blazer hung loosely from his shoulders, and his tie was unknotted, the first button of his light gray shirt undone. He looked awfully young to be a detective, Sadie thought.

"Do you happen to know who the person is who discovered the body?" he asked.

"That would be me," Sadie said.

"I have a few questions for you, if you don't mind." Cross pulled a small notebook and a pen out of his blazer pocket and clicked the pen.

"I've already told Detective Frogert everything I saw. I'd really like to go home. I promise I'll find time to come to the station to make a formal statement if I need to."

Keith touched Sadie's shoulder. "No, ma'am. I'm not with the police. I'm with a local online newsfeed. I was listening to the police scanner when I heard about a body at the Wainwright mansion."

"What?" Sadie's head began to pound as hard as her heart. "Don't you work with Detective Frogert?"

"No, ma'am. I'm a reporter. Would you be willing to tell me what you saw? I'm sure you must be in shock, but my job is to report crime in the city. Will you help me?"

Sadie looked into Keith Cross's face. "I wish I could help you. I can't even help myself. I need to go home. Now."

Sadie pushed past the beautiful young man to her car, strapped Coco in safely, climbed into the driver's side, turned on the ignition, and sped away. In her rearview mirror, she saw Keith Cross waving at her. She hoped never to see him again. Having accidentally given him her name, however, she feared she would.

FOUR

As she drove away from the Wainwright mansion, Sadie debated where to go. Home sounded appealing, but too much had happened to sit alone, no offense to Coco, of course. Sometimes circumstances called for human interaction.

Amber was in the process of closing the shop when Sadie arrived. The front door was already locked, the last customer gone. Sadie used her store key to let herself in and then locked the door behind her. She spotted Amber in the back of the shop, tidying the dressing rooms in preparation for the next day.

"How did it go?" Amber called out. "Did you and Roberta get some decorating done?"

Sadie got Coco situated on her usual velvet countertop pillow and sighed as Amber approached with an armload of go-backs. "Not exactly."

Amber gave Sadie a concerned look. "You look exhausted and upset. What is it?"

"You're not going to believe this." Sadie slumped onto the stool they kept behind the register and pushed a loose hair off her forehead with the back of her hand. "Roberta's dead."

"What?" Amber dropped the armload of clothes on the counter, and the hangers clattered as they hit the surface. "Oh, Sadie! What happened?"

"I don't know. No one knows. I just found her on the floor

of the ballroom."

"*You* found her? I'm so sorry," Amber said. "That must have been terrible. What did you do? I would have been hysterical."

"I think I was too shocked to be hysterical. I called the police immediately, of course, and then I left the building. There's no way I was going to stay inside. I sat on the front steps until they arrived."

Amber nodded. "I'm sure I would have done the same thing. Did they arrive quickly?"

"Yes, thank goodness," Sadie said. She shivered, remembering the dreadful feeling of waiting alone. "And guess who showed up when they arrived?"

"I have no idea... Oh, wait!" Amber's eyes grew wide. "You've got to be kidding. Froggy?"

"None other."

Coco yawned, as if knowing the entire episode was about to unfold again. Sadie pulled a treat from a jar on a back shelf and gave it to the Yorkie, after which she lowered her head onto the velvet pillow and ignored the continuing conversation.

"Well, I'm guessing he was surprised to see you," Amber said.

Sadie huffed a pseudo laugh. "I certainly hope so. I don't relish the idea that law enforcement might start expecting to find me at murder scenes."

"That would be highly undesirable," Amber said, stating the obvious. "And you do seem to have a pattern of doing that." She began to pick up the scattered hangers and clothing she'd dropped on the counter. One by one, she straightened them and hung them on a side rack usually used for hold items.

A tap on the front door caused both Sadie and Amber to jump, their nerves on edge from the shocking events.

"It's Matteo," Amber said. "He must have just closed up shop. Should I let him in?"

"Only if he comes bearing chocolate," Sadie said. "I'm kidding, of course. Let him in. I'll end up telling him all this anyway."

Amber took the keys and let Matteo in. Sure enough, he did carry a box from Cioccolato, which he placed on the counter. He took one look at Sadie and frowned.

"You look exhausted and upset," he said.

"So I've been told," Sadie said, eyeing the box.

"I said the same thing when she walked in." Amber lifted the lid off the box, and both she and Sadie surveyed the contents.

"Today's mishaps," Matteo said. "Perfect in taste but lacking the aesthetic quality necessary for the display case."

"You can never have too many mishaps for me," Sadie said as she picked out a lopsided truffle. "And I can use them today."

"Rough day?"

Sadie nodded. "I unexpectedly ended up at a murder scene," she said, her speech slightly garbled by a mouth full of chocolate.

"Again?"

Amber and Matteo exchanged glances, and Amber nodded.

"Yes, again," Sadie said. "And this time was very upsetting. I happened to be the person to find her, which is quite different than being a bystander after the fact."

"Her?" Matteo repeated.

"Roberta Wainwright," Amber said.

"Roberta Wainwright?" Matteo's expression was incredulous. "Why, I just spoke with her yesterday. She ordered a huge platter of ghost-themed chocolates for the event this weekend."

"I wonder if they'll even have it now," Amber said.

"I have no idea." Sadie took another misfit chocolate from the box, this one oozing caramel from a split on the side. "The police are still at the scene. I drove here straight from there." She popped the sweet confection in her mouth.

"Maybe it'll be called off," Amber said.

"That would certainly be understandable considering the circumstances," Sadie said. "Still, unfortunate. The Spooktacular raises so much money for charities."

Matteo nodded. "Yes, I read in the *Chronicle* that this year's event is expected to have the biggest turnout the Wainwright mansion has ever seen, based on the advance ticket sales. I was excited that Cioccolato would have a presence there, though that seems trivial compared to what has happened."

Sadie replaced the lid on the chocolates as Coco began to sniff her way toward the box. "I'm sorry, Coco. You know chocolate isn't good for you." She picked up the dog and cuddled her against her chest while reaching for her tote bag. "I should get home. I suppose I need to find out if the event is canceled or not."

"You have Roberta's number," Amber suggested. "But..."

"I don't think she'll answer," Sadie said absentmindedly. "Not to make light of the situation," she added quickly. "And I wouldn't want to bother family members. Not at a time like this." She hoped she hadn't sounded insensitive and wondered if the shock of the day was causing her to speak before thinking. All the more reason to head home.

"Take the misfit chocolates with you. I have a feeling you could use them tonight." Matteo picked up the box and handed it to Sadie, who gladly accepted the offering once Coco was situated inside the tote. Matteo bid both women goodbye and left.

"When you get home, you should rest, Sadie." Amber gave Sadie a friendly squeeze on one shoulder. "Try to relax and get your mind off this if you can."

Sadie had no hesitation accepting the suggestion. "You're absolutely right. This has been a long, stressful day. I believe I see a warm bath and a hot cup of tea in my near future."

"Are you going to call Broussard and tell him what's going on?" Amber asked, referring to Sadie's long-distance beau in New Orleans.

"I will but maybe not tonight," Sadie said. "I just don't know if I can bear rehashing this again right now. I'll probably wait until tomorrow to call him."

With that, Sadie left Amber to finish closing up the shop. Driving from Flair to her penthouse apartment, she knew her yearning for a quiet evening of relaxation was the best plan. She had no doubt at all that the next day would bring some sort of new commotion.

FIVE

Early-morning light streamed in through Sadie's bedroom window as a dull buzz caused her to open her eyes. Coco stirred sleepily as Sadie inched closer to the edge of the bed in order to grab her phone off the nightstand. She was not surprised to hear Amber on the other end of the line, trying to convince her to stay home to rest and recover from the shock of finding Roberta's body.

"I can handle everything," Amber said, "and if something comes up, Matteo will be next door to help out. You deserve a day off after everything you went through yesterday."

Sadie had to admit the offer was tempting, but she had paperwork to catch up on, and she and Amber had plans to set sale prices for upcoming specials. "No, no, I'm fine. It will do me good to come in. I need the distraction. Besides, don't you have a lunch date with Dylan? I remember it being his day off." She could practically hear Amber blush through the phone.

While Sadie appreciated Amber's encouragement to stay home, Sadie knew she wouldn't be able to relax. She'd either pace her apartment or go hunting for clues to Roberta's murder. Pacing her apartment never appealed to her, especially since pacing annoyed Coco, and she could hear Broussard tsking in her ear *Do* not *get involved in this investigation.* It was one reason she'd decided not to call her New Orleans detective the night before. She would call him, of course. She just wasn't quite ready to yet.

Once she arrived at Flair, Sadie was glad she'd decided to come in for the day. Receiving orders, pricing the sales items, and being with Amber all soothed her frazzled nerves. She could barely admit to herself that she'd spent most of the night fighting off nightmares of seeing Roberta's body, her face covered with a sequined mask, the chandelier on her head, the sound of glass shattering over and over. Sadie was made of hardy stock, and she didn't usually give in to what she considered the "vapors." But this was different. Roberta hadn't exactly been a friend, as she'd told Froggy, but she was someone Sadie had known for several years. A good customer, tolerable enough if a bit too quick to show off her wealth.

She suspected she'd call Broussard that evening. She wasn't sure why she'd hesitated the night before, aside from anticipating his reaction. Was there more to it than that? Their relationship was new and, as such, not yet defined. Were they on that path where he would be the one she turned to for comfort? Maybe. She found him more than comforting.

Around twelve thirty, Dylan stopped by to pick up Amber for their lunch date.

"Are you sure you'll be all right alone?" Amber asked, one hand on her purse, the other reaching for Dylan's hand.

"I'll be fine. It's not like anyone is going to drop a chandelier on my head in the middle of the shop here." Sadie looked up at the rather ordinary drop ceiling tiles. "Besides, Matteo is next door if I need him, and I have Froggy's card. I'll be perfectly safe."

And she meant it. She was used to spending time alone in the shop. But after the door shut behind Amber and her new beau, Sadie had to admit she was uneasy.

"I don't know, Coco," she said to the sweet dog sleeping on the counter. "Something about this one feels different. It feels more… personal?"

She thought about calling Broussard without waiting until the evening, but she knew he was probably busy with a string of burglaries in the French Quarter or some other sort of Big Easy crime spree. She would hold off until later when she could relax in her favorite silk pajamas, a cool glass of chardonnay beside her.

"I know what we need, Coco. We need lunch. How about a sandwich from Giabaldi's?"

Coco raised her head and opened one sleepy eye. The word *sandwich* always caught her interest.

"Grilled mozzarella on sourdough with tomato basil soup. They'll add a pickle and warmed chips. Oh, and a sweet, sweet iced tea. Perfect." Sadie practically sang the order to the empty store, so excited at the thought of her favorite deli's food.

She called in the order, and while she waited for delivery, she printed price tags for a new shipment of linen jackets they'd received the day before, then moved on to other shop tasks. She'd told Amber to take her time with Dylan. Amber was so congenial when it came to filling in for Sadie when she needed to run out of town for the day—or to, well, investigate things—that letting the young assistant manager have some extra time for a romantic lunch was the least Sadie could do.

Sadie was deep in a rack of long, glittering skirts when the bell to the store's door jangled.

"Be right with you!" she called. "Feel free to look around!"

"I just have a lunch order," a girl's voice said. "I'll put it on the counter."

"Oh, wonderful!" Sadie popped up from the rack of clothing and headed to the front. "How much do I owe you?"

"Fourteen fifty," the girl said. She was tiny, a little brunette of a woman, wearing a yellow ball cap and jeans with holes in the knees. "That sandwich is my favorite."

"It's the most splendid sandwich in the deli," Sadie agreed. "And that soup is divine." She handed the girl a twenty-dollar bill and took the sweet iced tea from the girl's other hand. "Keep the change!"

"Oh, thank you so much!"

As the girl was leaving, Sadie heard someone else enter, and she regretted for a moment that she hadn't turned the sign hanging on the doorknob to read CLOSED for a few minutes. She was aching to fill her belly, and the aroma of melted cheese and fresh basil was intoxicating.

When she looked up, she found herself bewildered. The man who had entered was not the typical Flair customer. Even her male customers had a certain style. A wealthy air, tailored suits, polished shoes. Sadie wasn't a snob by any means. But she'd never quite had a customer like this one. She set her lunch on a shelf below the counter and came out into the center of the shop.

"Can I help you find something?"

"I think maybe you're what I came to find," the man said. His voice was deep and melodic.

"Oh?" Sadie thought about reaching for her cell phone to call Matteo next door, in case she needed help. But she knew her experience at the mansion was making her more nervous than usual. She often handled single customers on her own, and there was nothing in the man's tone of voice or odd appearance to indicate he was dangerous.

Sadie wasn't accustomed to being the object of someone's attention. She was used to being the person who studied people, observed, and investigated.

"What do you mean I'm what you're looking for?" she asked the sad, drooping man. Everything about him reeked of sorrow from his hat to the dusty Dr. Martens on his feet.

The man was tall, probably close to six five. He was rangy and lean, and she would have thought he reminded her of a cowboy except for the pork pie hat perched on top of his head. The only word she could think of to describe his attire was *shabby*.

"My name is Guy Bijou." He pulled a business card out of his wallet and handed it to Sadie. "I'm a paranormal investigator. Perhaps you're a fan of my show?"

Sadie looked at the card. GUY'S GHOSTS AND GOBLINS, the card read, along with the slogan IS IT A GHOST OR A GOBLIN? The address was in New Orleans, the logo a trio of *G*s with each letter warped into a ghoulish shape. She couldn't decide whether it was creepy or cool, finally settling on a mix of each.

Sadie laid the card on top of the counter. Coco left her plush bed to sniff the small rectangle, then coughed a doggie cough. "I'm afraid I haven't," Sadie said, the admission eliciting a mixed look of surprise and disappointment on the man's face. "What did you want to talk to me about? Do you have a lady ghost friend who needs an outfit?" She regretted the taunting question the instant it left her mouth.

Guy rolled his shoulders forward and pulled his hat lower onto his head. "I do, actually, have a lady friend who might appreciate your boutique. But I really wanted to talk to you about a haunted mansion. The Wainwright mansion, to be exact."

Sadie's stomach did a flip-flop. "Why me?" Again, she casually reached for the phone.

"I read about you on San Francisco Unlocked," Guy said. "You know, that news website that covers the most unusual aspects of this city along with regular stuff like city government, crime, and zoning issues. Your name came up as the person who discovered Roberta Wainwright's body in the Wainwright mansion, and I knew I had to talk to you."

Sadie hadn't heard anything about being on the news and could only surmise that the man she'd mistaken for a police officer when leaving the mansion, Keith Cross, had published an account of the murder. She wondered how ethical it was for the young reporter to release the name of a private citizen who had experienced a terrible trauma.

"What if I don't want to talk to you?" Sadie kept the counter between her and Guy Bijou. She still didn't sense that he was dangerous, but she wasn't taking any chances. Coco was emitting an odd sound, a cross between a growl and what Sadie would swear was a purr if Coco had been a cat.

"I understand, Ms. Kramer. I'm sure the event was traumatic for you. But please, I need your help."

"Doesn't everybody these days?" she muttered.

The man shuffled nervously from one foot to the other. "I've had a bit of a financial setback with my show. You know, it's been really popular, and over the years, I've done a lot of good for people whose properties have been infested with spirits. I had a bit of a controversy last year, and my show is in jeopardy. I've been in the Bay area for the past few days, investigating various haunted venues, and I heard about the, er, death in San Francisco. I need just one true ghost tale to get me back on track, and I think the Wainwright Ghost is the ticket to my renewed success." Guy pulled the hat off his head and twirled it between his hands.

"The Wainwright Ghost? You think a ghost killed Roberta Wainwright?" Sadie shook her head. "There are no such things as ghosts." Sadie laid a hand on Coco's back, surprised to find the dog was trembling. Was she afraid of this man, or was she drawn to him? There was no way to know unless Coco decided between biting and licking.

"Well, I've encountered a few ghosts in my day, but if you don't believe in ghosts, what do you think about goblins?"

Sadie snorted. "That's even more ridiculous than the idea that ghosts exist. What are you going to tell me next? That vampires roam the earth, surviving on human blood?"

Guy dropped his hat, bent to pick it up, and put it back on his head. "I know this must sound crazy to you, ma'am. But I've spent my whole life studying the paranormal, trying to prove that there's just a thin veil between our living, human existence and what is beyond what we think of as death or the other side. Let me ask you one question about the moments when you were in the mansion. Please?"

"Oh, all right." Sadie kept her hand on Coco's back.

"Did you hear any weird noises, like shattering glass or wailing?"

"I did hear shattering glass, but no wailing."

"When you discovered the body"—Guy paused for a moment and chewed on his lower lip—"was there a lot of broken glass or crystal in the room?"

Sadie stared at Guy as she processed his last question. Had the reporter been allowed inside the building? The police had not yet released a cause of death or description of the scene. "I don't think I should tell you what I saw."

"Can I tell you a ghost story? Or, well, it may be a goblin story."

Sadie sat down behind the counter and indicated that Guy should sit on a stool next to the counter but a few yards away. "Do you mind if I eat?" she asked.

"Not at all," Guy said.

"Then go ahead and tell me your ghost or goblin story." Sadie sipped her sweet tea and grimaced. The ice had melted and diluted it, and it tasted like sugar water. But her first bite into the sandwich was divine even though it was no longer warm.

"So it goes like this," Guy began. "The Wainwright mansion had a series of tragic incidents that haunted the family, about one every five years or so. In 1925, Amelia Wainwright, wife of the son of the man who built the mansion, died of mysterious circumstances in the ballroom just off the foyer."

Sadie dipped her plastic spoon into the lukewarm soup, tasted it, put the lid back on, and decided she would take it home and rewarm it for dinner. "What sort of circumstances?"

Guy eyed Sadie's bag of chips and licked his lips. "Here," she said. "Feel free." She handed him the bag. He crunched on a chip for a second, then continued.

"Amelia was planning an All Hallows' Eve extravaganza, a masquerade ball to beat all balls. She'd hired an orchestra, sent out invitations to all the elite of San Francisco, ordered all the guests to dress in costume, and hired the best chefs in the city to create the most exquisite finger foods."

"Sounds spectacular," Sadie said. Despite her skepticism, she was intrigued. Maybe her growing interest had something to do with Guy's sonorous voice.

"It would have been," Guy said as he helped himself to another chip. "But when the morning of the costume ball dawned, Amelia's housekeeper was checking the maids' work in the upstairs bedrooms when she heard a thud and a few moments later the sound of breaking glass."

Sadie suddenly grew cold though the store's thermostat was set at a comfortable seventy-five degrees. "Go on."

"The housekeeper ran downstairs and checked the dining room where tables adorned with white linen tablecloths, pumpkin center pieces, and polished silver waited for the guests to arrive. No one was in the room. She checked the front door and saw that it was open until a gust of wind blew it shut. She went to the back of the house where the large kitchen sat with steaming pots of food, trays of vegetables, and bottles of wine set on the sideboards. No one was there."

Sadie realized she was holding her breath. She was afraid to take another bite of her sandwich for fear of choking. "And then what happened?"

"The housekeeper finally noticed that the double doors to the ballroom were cocked open. When she stepped inside, she found the body of a woman lying on the floor, a glittering mask covering her face, the room's chandelier broken from its ceiling chain and lying like a crown just above Amelia's head. Because it was, of course, Amelia. The stories go that visitors sometimes hear the sound of glass shattering, wailing, and a kind of thud like something heavy has landed on a floor or the ground."

"How did you know about the way I found Roberta's body?" she said. "I didn't tell anyone, even that nosy reporter. The police saw it themselves, but they didn't tell anyone as far as I know. Why would they?"

"That's how you found Mrs. Wainwright?" Guy looked unapologetically triumphant.

"It is. But how did you know?"

"I didn't. It seems the legend is repeating itself," Guy said.

Sadie pulled the bag of chips toward her. "So you're saying a ghost killed Roberta Wainwright? A *ghost*?"

Guy shrugged. "They said it was more goblin than ghost, an angry little demon that clawed its way into our world from the other side, something spiteful and mean."

"So now you're telling me that a *goblin* killed Roberta Wainwright, not a ghost?"

"That's what makes this field so interesting!" Guy rubbed his hands together with enthusiasm. "Finding out the answer to the question 'Is it a ghost or a goblin?'"

Or a human being, Sadie thought to herself as she watched Guy Bijou adjust his hat, thank Sadie for the information and chips, and mosey out the front door.

SIX

Amber returned after lunch, bringing Dylan inside the shop with her. The two looked happy and peaceful in that particular way couples look when a relationship is new.

"How was lunch?"

"Great," Amber said. "Thanks for giving us extra time. We went down to the wharf for sourdough chowder bowls."

"Ah, one of my favorites," Sadie said. "Along with those shrimp cocktails."

"Were you okay here?" Amber asked. "Was it busy?"

"Not with customers, but I had an unusual visitor." Sadie picked up Guy Bijou's business card and handed it to Amber, who looked it over and then handed it to Dylan.

"A paranormal investigator?" Amber looked confused at first, then her eyes grew wide. "You see? I told you! There's more to that place than meets the eye."

"Hey," Dylan said, holding up the business card. "I know this show. I used to watch it all the time."

"Used to?" Sadie quirked an eyebrow.

"Sure, until it went on hiatus. Now the word is that it might be canceled." Dylan scratched his head. "Some kind of controversy about an episode in New Orleans."

"I see." Sadie bagged her soup container and remaining chips and set the half-consumed meal on the back counter. "What kind of controversy?"

"I don't remember exactly," Dylan said. "Someone died during filming, and I think her family accused the show of being rigged. There was some kind of argument between the producers about whose fault it was, and suddenly the show's future was left up in the air."

"Well, no matter," Sadie said, knowing exactly who to ask for that information. A call to Broussard could shed light on the specifics. "Why don't you two go on back out and enjoy your day together?"

"Are you sure?" Amber asked.

"Absolutely. It's very slow, and I can always use some quiet time to catch up on paperwork. I insist."

While Sadie enjoyed Amber's company immensely, she needed time alone to process what she'd experienced the day before as well as the odd visit from Guy Bijou. She knew she could do that better with just the company of Coco, who was a good listener to be sure and almost never interrupted Sadie's train of thought.

Amber and Dylan both thanked Sadie, grateful to have more time to spend together. After they departed, Sadie turned her attention to Coco.

"Considering the fact that we were in the thick of things, Coco, we don't know much about what really happened to Roberta." She took out a legal pad and a pencil and began to doodle. "One of the things that's intriguing me is that I believe Roberta might have been killed when we were in the mansion." Sadie shuddered. "I wish I'd gone straight in instead of wandering around the property first. Except..." The thought that she might have encountered a murderer was an unpleasant one.

She wrote down the words *chandelier, mask, necklace, double doors, thud.* She drew squiggly lines between the words and in the margins drew teardrop shapes that reminded her of the chandelier's crystals.

"Guy did mention that ghost story about a chandelier he said was tied to the house's history. Maybe someone tried to create a sort of copycat crime scene. What do you think, Coco?" The Yorkie yipped once at the sound of Guy's name, then curled up in a ball on top of the desk.

The shop phone rang, and Sadie answered. "Flair! Sadie speaking."

A voice that seemed oddly familiar breathed into Sadie's ear. "Did you say 'Flair'?"

"Yes," Sadie said, wondering who would call a store not knowing what store they were calling. A wrong number, perhaps. "This is Flair, the fashion boutique. What number were you trying to reach?"

"Well, I suppose this one. Are you Sadie Kramer?"

"Yes, yes I am."

"Oh, thank goodness! You could do me such a great service if you would consider helping me with preparations for the Spooktacular at the Wainwright mansion. We're so behind on setting up! And I can't seem to find the decorations UPS supposedly delivered, and now we have to…"

Caught off guard, Sadie broke in on the woman's frantic exhalation of panic and whispered, "Roberta?" As soon as the name slipped off her lips, she realized how ridiculous she was being. Guy's ghost stories must have affected her more than she realized.

"No. This is not Roberta. Roberta was my mother, and Roberta is dead."

"Oh my goodness!" Sadie felt horrible. "I'm so sorry. I must still be reeling from the aftereffects of the shock yesterday. I'm the one who found her, you see."

The person on the other end of the line, who sounded so eerily like Roberta, was silent.

"Are you still there?" Sadie asked.

"Yes. I'm still here. I'm Charlotte Wainwright, Roberta's daughter. I've been acting as her assistant on the event, and I found your name and number in her notes. I didn't realize you were the person who found her body." Charlotte cleared her throat, and Sadie was sure the poor girl was holding back tears. "I'm sorry you had to see that. All of us are in shock."

"Yes, I imagine your family must be stricken," Sadie said. "You're still going through with the event?"

"Absolutely! Mother would have wanted us to use the Spooktacular as a way to celebrate her life. And so many of the community's charities rely on this event that we felt we couldn't let them down despite our loss." Charlotte seemed to take a moment to regain her composure.

"It's going to be all right," Sadie said. It sounded like the right thing to say. "What can I do to help?"

"Anything would be fabulous. I just don't know how we'll get everything done now. My father is having trouble getting a flight back from Houston, and he'll have his own details to handle once he does get here. Is there any chance you could help tomorrow?"

Sadie put her hand over the phone's mouthpiece and sighed. What else could she do but agree to help? Maybe she'd end up learning something she could pass on to Froggy. There was no question she'd hear from him again. Most likely sooner rather than later. "Of course I can be there for you for whatever you need."

A sigh of relief came through the phone. "Great! I can't tell you how much I appreciate this. We won't have access inside yet, but the police said we can be outdoors, and there's plenty to do there. We just have to stay away from the mansion itself until they clear it."

"All right," Sadie said, not that the idea of walking back into the mansion felt right in any type of way. "What time do you need me there?"

"Come tomorrow, whenever you're able to get away from the store. I'll be there all day and probably around the clock until we open the doors to the public," Charlotte said. "There's just so much to do!"

"I'll be there in the morning," Sadie said. "I'll just need to give Amber a lunch break at the shop at some point."

Sadie and Charlotte exchanged cell phone numbers just in case one or the other of them got delayed, and the call ended. Putting her phone away, Sadie ran a gentle hand over Coco's head. "Well, Coco, I have a feeling tomorrow will be quite the adventure."

SEVEN

Sadie sighed as she dropped her keys on the kitchen counter. She lifted Coco out of her tote bag, setting her down to run freely inside the apartment. The dog made a beeline to her favorite toy in the living room, taking the stuffed red lobster with her as she curled up in a cozy dog bed near the couch.

Pouring a glass of wine—a chardonnay from the Tremiato Vineyards, a winery that had been in Matteo's family for generations—Sadie took a generous sip and placed the glass in the refrigerator to keep cool. She retired to the bedroom and exchanged her daytime clothes for a favorite chenille robe in a deep fuchsia shade.

A warm bath was next on her evening list, exactly what she needed to organize her thoughts for the text she planned to send to Broussard. She filled the tub, added a sparkling lavender bath bomb to the water, and hung the plush robe on a wall hook. Luxuriously she sank into the soothing bubbles and let her mind wander as her muscles relaxed.

The handsome New Orleans detective was bound to have questions. It was the nature of his job to be inquisitive. He was very good at solving puzzles, bringing together clues in a way that led to something others didn't see. She was quite sure he could give Froggy a run for his money, maybe even some tips for solving cases. So he was the perfect person to turn to regarding Roberta's sudden demise. And he might be able to provide some insight on Guy Bijou's paranormal investigation dealings as well.

However, he was unlikely to be thrilled to learn she had once again found herself at a murder scene. She was prepared for this reaction already, just as she was prepared to respond. It wasn't as if she planned these things. There were plenty of places she'd prefer to end up instead. Ghirardelli Square, for example. In Paris for a walk along the Seine. At a Broadway production. The list could go on and on. Nowhere would a murder scene be found.

Yet it had happened, and she would need to explain to Broussard how she ended up standing over a chandelier-crowned corpse when she'd only expected to help decorate an old mansion. The question was how to explain something she didn't understand herself. People collected all sorts of things—stamps, owl figurines, thimbles, and dozens of other items. Who on earth collected murder scenes?

Well, apparently I do. Sadie stepped out of the bathtub, dried off, and wrapped the cushy chenille robe around her. Retrieving her glass of wine from the refrigerator, she grabbed her cell phone and sat on the couch. She set the chardonnay on a side table and tapped a new text into the phone.

Detective Broussard.

There was no response at first, and Sadie wondered if he might be out on a police call of some sort. Although it was evening, and even later in New Orleans than in San Francisco, crime didn't tend to follow set office hours. Still, only a few minutes went by before her phone buzzed.

Ms. Kramer.

Sadie was fond of the formal way they addressed each other on first contact. It was formal in an informal way, or informal in a formal way. Something like that. It seemed like a reasonable way to start a conversation. Aside from an excuse to stall, of course. She was still debating how to explain the recent events.

How are you, Detective?

Fine, at least at the moment. Criminals seem to have taken a night off in NOLA.

Sadie looked at her phone, contemplating a response. She finally decided on a straightforward reply. *Good to hear. I wish that were the case here. There's been an unfortunate incident.*

There was a pause before a new text came through, which didn't surprise her in the least.

I'm afraid to ask.

Sadie sighed. He was planning to draw it out of her slowly. She might as well just spill it.

I told you I was going to help with a charity event, right? She knew he'd remember. She had shamelessly whined about wishing she hadn't volunteered. And now, more than ever, she truly wished she hadn't.

Yes, the Halloween fundraiser. Something went wrong? Did it get canceled?

Not exactly. I went to meet my customer, Roberta, and found her… Sadie froze, unable to type the word.

You found her and then what?

She could almost picture Broussard drumming his fingers against a desk or table or whatever piece of furniture he happened to be near.

Well, I found her, but she was dead. Sadie winced, and she wasn't at all surprised to see the text disappear, replaced immediately by an incoming phone call. She pressed the button to accept the call and lifted the phone to her ear.

"Detective Broussard."

"Ms. Kramer, expert of being in the wrong place at the wrong time."

Sadie took a sip of wine while trying to think of a witty response. She failed to come up with anything. Broussard had a point, one that had been proven more than once.

"Sadie?"

"Yes, yes, I'm here. I was trying to come up with something clever to say in return, but I came up empty-handed. Or empty-headed. Something like that. Maybe both." She could hear a faint chuckle on the other end of the line and could picture the smirk that surely accompanied it. A handsome smirk, admittedly.

"How about we skip clever and just go for straight information?" Broussard suggested.

"I can do that," Sadie said, breathing a sigh of relief. It was a much better option than getting the lecture she'd imagined. "I went to meet Roberta at the Wainwright mansion to help with decorations."

"Yesterday at two, right? I recall that's when you said you were going to go."

"Yes, except she called me that morning, asking me to come at noon instead."

"Interesting," Broussard said. "How did she sound when she called?"

She hadn't thought much about it at the time, but she could see why he was asking. "She sounded frantic."

"Frantic?"

"She couldn't find some decorations that were supposed to have been delivered."

"And she wanted you to come early to help find them?"

Sadie thought that over, recalling the rushed phone conversation. "I suppose. She didn't say. I just agreed to meet her earlier. But I can understand why she'd be panicking if she couldn't find the delivery."

"Why is that?"

"It's a huge mansion. Getting it ready for the event would be a big job even after everything needed was laid out and organized. It never crossed my mind that anything else might be wrong." Sadie wondered suddenly if she'd missed something in the phone call that she should have caught. Or that would have helped if she had. No, she reassured herself. Roberta had simply expressed frustration at not being able to find the decorations.

"Who else was there when you arrived?"

"No one."

"What do you mean no one?"

Sadie could hear the worry in his voice, but there was no other answer to give. "I mean exactly that. This wasn't a committee meeting or anything like that. We were just getting together to organize some decorations.

"So, you're the one who *found* her?" Broussard exhaled. "Sadie, I'm so sorry. That type of scene is upsetting even to those of us who've seen it more times than we care to remember."

"It was… terrible." Sadie shivered just thinking about it.

"You don't have to tell me," Broussard said. "I'm sure recounting it is difficult. Let's skip that part for now. I'm assuming you called the police and were questioned when they arrived."

"Yes," Sadie said. "And you'll never believe who showed up. Detective Frogert."

"I see," Broussard replied. "Interesting turn of events. Did anyone else surprising show up?"

Sadie remembered the Jaguar that had squealed to a stop

in front of the mansion, the noise as clear in her head as the sound of shattering glass. "Yes, Cooper Wainwright, Roberta's son, was there."

"Wait. You said the mansion was empty when you went to meet Roberta." Broussard sounded more like a detective and less like a friend.

"It *was* empty. Cooper came by after the police got there. He told me the caretaker would normally have been in the building and thought his mother would have been safe if Dwight hadn't taken the day off."

"And what were you doing talking to the son of the dead woman?" Broussard asked.

Sadie remained quiet.

"Ms. Kramer? Are you still there?"

"I didn't seek out Cooper, you know. He started talking to me. Am I being interrogated now, Detective Broussard?"

"Sorry, it's a habit." Sadie could hear a touch of humor in Broussard's voice. "Anything else going on?"

"Yes. Today, in fact," Sadie said. "A man who claims to be a paranormal investigator came by the store, asking questions."

"That seems a little odd." Broussard sounded concerned. "Did he leave his name? I can run a check on him."

"He left a card. Strange guy, but he seemed harmless. He runs—or ran, I can't get the story straight—a television show called *Ghosts and Goblins.*"

Broussard was silent.

"Are you still there?" Sadie asked. This conversation felt a bit like a ping-pong match.

"I'm here. And I'm quite familiar with that show, as well as with Guy Bijou. That's who this is, right?"

"Yes, exactly."

"We had a case here that he was involved with."

"Some kind of show scandal, right?"

"How did you know? Ghost-hunting shows don't seem like your style."

"They're not. Amber's boyfriend, Dylan, is a fan and told me about it."

"I'll call Frogert and see what I can find out. Maybe the Guy Bijou case here would be of interest to him."

"Should I be worried about this investigator?" Sadie asked, suddenly concerned. "He seemed a nice enough guy—no pun intended." She winced at her choice of words.

"I've met him and spoken with him several times. He doesn't strike me as dangerous. But you should always be careful with strangers. With anyone, really, Sadie."

"Is this where I say, 'Thank you, Dad?'"

"Very funny." She could hear Broussard chuckle in spite of trying to remain serious. "You'll find out most of what you want to know about that show on the internet."

"Great suggestion. It'll help take my mind off Roberta."

"There you go." Broussard's voice softened. "I'll give you a call after I talk to... I believe you call him Froggy?"

Again, Sadie heard him chuckle. She knew the question was rhetorical, so she didn't answer.

"Thank you for filling me in. Sleep well. It's great to hear your voice, Ms. Kramer."

"Yours too, Detective Broussard."

EIGHT

When Sadie pulled up to park in front of the Wainwright mansion the next morning, three cars were already there: Cooper's golden Jaguar, a small sky-blue SUV, and the little compact with the dented fender. Sadie saw that it was a dull silver, but she didn't know its make. She tucked Coco into her tote bag, draped it over her arm, and stepped onto the Wainwright property. As she expected, police tape blocked the entrance to the mansion itself. But the pathways through the garden and out toward the orchard were clear.

Partway down the main path to the orchard, she could hear two voices: one, a man's, the other, a woman's. She easily recognized Cooper's voice from her first conversation with him. The second voice clearly matched the one on the phone call she'd received at the shop. It belonged to Roberta's daughter, Charlotte. Sadie followed the sound of the conversation.

"I cannot *believe* you're going ahead with this stupid party after what happened to Mom! It's disrespectful. You're as coldhearted as she was!"

Sadie stopped just outside the orchard. She didn't want to interrupt what sounded like an intimate and emotional discussion between grieving siblings. Also, she thought, she might hear something useful if they didn't realize she was there.

"Don't you dare bad-mouth her now," Charlotte shouted. "And this 'stupid' party was the highlight of her year! She would be appalled to think of what would happen to all those projects that need funding if we didn't open our doors to donors!"

"You don't *really* care about honoring Mother. You just want those donations for your own pet charities, including that ridiculous graveyard cleanup project. No one cares about dead people!"

Sadie pressed her fingers against her mouth. She wondered if Cooper realized how what he'd just said sounded.

"And what about you?" Charlotte shrieked. "You don't care about any of these causes. You never have. You'd rather use that money for your precious cars, old run-down houses, and swanky apartments!"

Sadie heard a sound that reminded her of the thud that was Roberta's falling body, and she wondered if brother had pushed sister over or if sister had shoved brother. She took a few quiet steps backward and was about to announce her presence to the young people when someone tapped her on the shoulder.

Sadie was amazed that she didn't scream. Coco, however, was not as disciplined and let out one of her expressive series of yips. When Sadie turned, she expected to see either one of the Wainwright siblings, if not both. Instead, she looked up into Guy Bijou's melancholy face.

"Sorry to startle you." Guy looked down as if he couldn't quite stand to peer directly into Sadie's eyes.

"What are you doing here?" Sadie asked, instinctively taking a step back.

The argument had stopped, and Sadie could hear the sound of footsteps approaching.

"I was only planning to drive by the mansion, but I saw the cars out front, so I figured it couldn't hurt if I took a small peek inside. But of course it's taped off."

"So here you are," Sadie said.

Guy looked up from the ground as if Sadie's statement affirmed his presence. "Yes, that's right. Here I am."

Cooper and a tall, lanky brunette, who looked like a stretched, younger version of Roberta, stepped out from behind a cluster of trees. The woman silently took notice of Sadie and then pointed her finger at Guy. "And just who are *you*?"

Before Guy had a chance to speak up, Cooper answered the question for him.

"Wait, I know who you are," he said, eyeing Guy with suspicion. "You're from that television show. *Ghosts and Goblins*. I used to watch it all the time. That is, I did until…"

Guy cleared his throat. "Yes, well it's actually *Guy's Ghosts and Goblins*, and I'm delighted you enjoyed the show. Hopefully, it will be back on the air soon."

"I'm Cooper Wainwright, and this is my sister, Charlotte."

"Guy Bijou." Guy reached out to shake hands with Cooper and Charlotte. Cooper obliged with a quick palm-to-palm touch, but Charlotte ignored Guy's hand altogether. He wiped it on the back of his jeans and shoved it into his jacket pocket. "Sorry to intrude," he said. "I didn't think anyone from the family would be here. I'm so sorry for your loss. I know what it's like to lose a parent."

Sadie eyed Guy. She rather wished he'd stop talking. When Coco popped her head out of the tote and growled at no one in particular, Sadie assumed the little dog agreed.

"It's nice to see you again, Ms. Kramer," Cooper said.

"Please call me Sadie. I hope you're feeling a bit better today."

Cooper nodded. "I am, thank you."

Sadie turned to Charlotte. "It's so nice to meet you in person. How can I help?"

Charlotte approached Sadie and seemed about to link arms with her when a light, clear voice called out from behind the mansion.

"Charlotte? Is everything all right? I thought I heard shouting. I just finished going over the lighting plans for the back garden with Dwight. I'm coming over now."

"Everything is fine, Maggie," Charlotte called in return.

The woman who appeared carrying a clipboard was in her late thirties or early forties with chin-length black hair that swung into her face as if the edges were weighted. She looked slightly familiar to Sadie, or perhaps it was her outfit that did. The grayish-blue skirt and fitted jacket looked a lot like something Flair had carried. In fact, hadn't Amber sold that exact outfit recently?

"What you heard, Maggie dear," Cooper said, "was the sound of sibling rivalry echoing through the trees." He took Maggie's free hand and air-kissed the knuckles. "We're fine. It was no big deal. Isn't that right?" He released her hand and turned to Charlotte, who smiled perfunctorily. Cooper mimicked her smile and then turned to Guy. "I think my sister would appreciate it if I left her to party preparations. She has Sadie to help her now."

Sadie could swear she heard a hint of bitterness in his voice. "Only if it's no bother," she said quickly, feeling a heavy dose of family tension in the air. "I could come back at a different time if that's better. I'm sure you have plenty of family business to discuss…"

"Of course it's not a bother," Charlotte chirped with a tone Sadie pegged as sounding exactly like that of her recently departed mother. "I need all the help I can get at this point." She gestured for Sadie to follow her.

Cooper, seemingly dismissed by the females, turned to Guy. "I don't know if your being in town just days after Mother's death is a coincidence or what, but come have a beer with me." He pointed to a shady spot under a tree several rows back. Two folding chairs flanked a red-and-white cooler. "I'd love to interrogate you about your show and about why you happened to turn up at the mansion."

Guy looked startled, and he glanced at Sadie as if she could help him get out of the invitation. She shrugged. Coco barked once, always willing to back Sadie up.

"Well, that's nice of you," Guy said, "but isn't it a bit early for a drink?"

"Soda or a bottle of cold water then. We have lots of choices. Come on, man," Cooper insisted. "Let's leave the decorating to the women." He placed his hand on Guy's back and ushered him toward the chairs.

"That Guy person seems a bit strange," Charlotte said once the men were out of hearing range. "Why did you bring him with you, Sadie?" She led the way down the path toward several cartons waiting in the shade of the orchard.

"I didn't. He just happened to drive by." Sadie followed Charlotte. Maggie walked a few steps behind while scanning the top sheet on her clipboard.

"But you know him?" Charlotte walked over to one of the boxes and pulled out an assortment of decorations Sadie assumed would hang from tree branches.

"I suppose so," Sadie said. "But I only met him yesterday when he stopped by my shop, so I don't really *know* him. He says he's a paranormal investigator, has his own television show. I guess San Francisco is full of ghosts."

Charlotte huffed. "Well, his timing couldn't be worse. Showing up coincidentally right after someone is murdered? My brother is right to be suspicious."

The black-haired woman cleared her throat. She looked over some kind of paper or form on her clipboard that Sadie couldn't quite see.

"I'm sorry, Charlotte, if you could just sign this, I can make sure the caterer gets paid."

"Of course, Maggie. Sorry to keep you waiting." She took the clipboard and signed without reading it. "I know you must be buried under paperwork and phone calls."

"I am, but it's fine, of course! It's better this way." She took the clipboard back from Charlotte. "I really must go. I have a noon meeting with the attorneys, and some detective named Frog something or other left me a message."

"Oh, you must mean Detective Frogert," Sadie said. "I spoke to him the day..." She trailed off as Maggie turned away and headed for the street.

"Yes, well. Sorry to have to run," Maggie called over her shoulder. "So much to take care of!" She left the property almost at a trot.

"It's too bad she ran off before I could introduce you," Charlotte said. "Maggie Barton is the Wainwright Foundation's executive director. She isn't usually that brusque."

"Don't even worry about it," Sadie said. "Can I ask you something?"

"Sure." Charlotte waited as if Sadie were about to interrogate her.

"It's nothing important, really. I just wanted to know who drives the little silver car I saw parked out front."

"Oh, that belongs to our caretaker. I don't know why it's upfront. He usually keeps it parked in one of the garages behind the mansion." She glanced around the orchard. "Why don't we open these boxes to see what we have?"

They each began opening the several boxes stacked neatly on the grass. Something about the earlier argument versus the calm of the garden seemed to make the two women relish the quiet, though they could hear the soft murmuring of Cooper and Guy chatting in the distance. They worked silently for a long time until Coco jumped out of her tote bag and ran to tug on a length of black fabric.

"Coco! Stop!" Sadie gently removed the cloth from Coco's mouth and glanced at her watch. "Oh dear," she said. "It's a quarter past twelve, and I promised Amber, my assistant, that I'd return to the store to give her a break for lunch. I have to go, but I'll be back after that." Charlotte stood from where she'd been crouched over a box of little ghosts, and Sadie saw how panicked she looked. "Don't worry!" she said. "I promise you we'll get everything done."

NINE

When Sadie entered the store, Amber was helping a lone customer, who was rifling through a stack of mohair sweaters, pulling one out that was a deep ocean blue. Sadie stopped next to the two women. "That's one of my favorite colors," she said. "And I think it matches your eyes!"

"Really?"

"Absolutely."

The customer hugged the sweater to her chest, thanked both Sadie and Amber for their help, and moved on to look through a rack of rhinestone-studded jeans.

Amber returned to the front counter, and Sadie followed. "How are things over at Wainwright mansion?" Amber asked.

"Fine," Sadie said. "Certainly less eventful than my last trip there, thank goodness."

"I should hope so! Are you really going back to the mansion this afternoon? Isn't it creepy? I don't think I could do it."

"We aren't working inside since the police haven't cleared the building yet, so it's not too awful." Sadie picked up a binder that lay on the counter. "I do want to get in some work before I have to go back. Are the latest purchase orders in here?"

"They are. I just finished filing them this morning," Amber said. "And they're updated in the computer system as well."

"Great," Sadie said. "And thank you! You're always so efficient. I have no idea what I'd do without you!"

The conversation paused while the customer brought the blue sweater to the counter. Amber rang up the sale and thanked her for coming in. Sadie echoed the sentiment, and the woman left the store.

"Don't you think it's strange that Roberta's daughter decided to go ahead with the Spooktacular?" Amber said. "It seems kind of cold to me that she'd just keep right on going. I mean, she just lost her mother."

Sadie tilted her head to one side much like Coco did when she was listening to Sadie dissect a case. "She seems to think the event will honor her mother's memory. I suppose it will help her through her grieving."

"Maybe. I guess I can see that." Amber looked skeptical. "I'll be back soon." She waved over her shoulder and left the shop.

Sadie settled Coco on top of the counter pillow and set down the binder. She sat on the front stool and looked around the store, filled with a kind of comfort that comes from routine. "Let's check the delivery windows on these orders," she said, patting Coco's head.

She had barely started to look over the first order sheet when the door jingled. She looked up to see that Seymour Wainwright had entered. He looked both dapper and sad, and his height made him tower above the counter. Sadie shook his proffered hand.

"I'm so very sorry about Roberta," Sadie said. "You must be devastated."

"Well, yes. I'm crushed," Seymour said. "And I'm furious. I can't understand why someone would kill Roberta. Everyone loved her."

Sadie wasn't quite sure that was true, but she knew people tended not to want to speak ill of the dead, as the saying goes. "Maybe it was some sort of accident," Sadie said, thinking somehow that the thought might be comforting.

"No, no. Absolutely not." Seymour shook his head firmly. "The detective tells me it was murder all right. But they won't tell me *how* she died yet. You were there, weren't you."

That was not a question. "I was, yes." The image of Roberta's masked face swam before Sadie's eyes, and she closed them against the memory.

"You're the one who found her," Seymour whispered. "I saw your name in a story on that news site, San Francisco Unlocked. It must have been horrible."

"It was." Sadie reached below the counter for a packet of tissues. Seymour didn't seem like the weepy type, but you never knew how someone would react to this sort of tragedy.

He covered his face with his hands. "My poor, dear Roberta. I should never have left her to handle the Spooktacular all on her own. I offered to cancel my business trip. She insisted she'd be fine. But if I'd been with her, this couldn't have happened."

A thought came unbidden into Sadie's head. *If I hadn't dawdled outside, admiring the landscaping, this might not have happened.* But if she'd gone into the mansion a little earlier, she, too, could have been a victim. She shook her head. She couldn't think that way.

"Mr. Wainwright, is there something I can do to help you?"

Seymour looked up at Sadie. "Please call me Seymour. Everyone is being so formal with me. It's unnerving."

"All right, Seymour it is."

"My son, Cooper, tells me you were at the mansion that morning to help Roberta with preparations for the

Spooktacular. He said you were very kind to him after the police wouldn't let him see his mother. So thank you for that." Seymour took a cigar out of the breast pocket of his suit coat and rolled it between his fingers.

"You're most welcome," Sadie said, hoping he wasn't planning to light the cigar right then and there. "It was quite a shock for both of us, but I'm glad your boy didn't have to see Roberta that way."

"May I ask you…?" Seymour looked at his cigar as if contemplating his question.

"Ask me anything."

"Was anyone else in the mansion when you arrived?"

Sadie shook her head. "No. When I called out to Roberta, no one answered, so I believe the building was empty except for us. I didn't find anyone on the other floors either."

"I wonder where Dwight was. He's the caretaker."

"Your son mentioned he had the day off."

"She shouldn't have been alone." Seymour tugged on his lower lip. "I understand you've offered to help Charlotte now that she's stepped into my wife's role as the coordinator?" He put the cigar back in his pocket, and Sadie wondered if he used it as a touchstone or charm.

"Yes," Sadie said. "Since I'd already agreed to help Roberta, it only seemed right to help Charlotte. She sounded pretty panicked when she called to ask."

"Charlotte's a good girl, but this isn't her usual schtick. She's helped every year since she was old enough, of course, but she's never been in charge. Maggie, that's the foundation's executive director, would have been a better coordinator. I thought we might all agree to cancel the Spooktacular, but I suppose my daughter is right. We can use the party to celebrate Roberta's life."

"I think it's admirable of your daughter to keep it going," Sadie said. "And it does help fund a lot of charities."

"Yes, well, that part is nice, I suppose." Seymour reached for the cigar again but didn't take it out this time. "I do think this may be the last one of these we do. I can't see it going on without Roberta's special touch. It really was her pet project." Seymour stepped back, and Sadie realized once again that he was quite tall, nearly as tall as Guy Bijou. He reached out to shake Sadie's hand again, which he covered with both of his. "Thank you for speaking to me, Sadie. I really just needed to see the person who was so kind to my wife and my son. And now, it seems, my daughter too."

"Again, you're welcome. And if there's anything I can do for you, please feel free to stop by again. Or to call."

Seymour nodded and left Sadie to gaze down at Coco, who had been sitting quietly on her pillow throughout the entire conversation.

Sadie returned to the purchase orders and was on the second when the shop door opened again and Frogert stepped in. Coco stood up on the pillow, staring at the detective. He reached out and hesitantly patted the dog on top of her head. Coco repaid his attempt to be affectionate with a quick lick, and Frogert withdrew his hand quickly. The Yorkie turned away from him and settled back down on the pillow.

"Hello, Detective," Sadie said. "Would you like some coffee? Water? A truffle?"

He stood in the same space Seymour had so recently abandoned, leaned on the counter with one arm, and loosened his tie with the other. "No, thank you. I'll get right to the point. What can you tell me about Guy Bijou?" He pulled a small notebook and pen out of his jacket pocket.

"You've been talking to Detective Broussard again, haven't

you?" Of course, she already knew Broussard had planned to call him, but there was no reason to say so.

He smiled and ran his finger over his mustache, which was no more developed than it had been three days before. The gesture irked Sadie as much as it had the first time he'd done it. "Detective Broussard and I have developed a strong professional friendship."

"How nice for you." Sadie picked up a pencil and began to doodle on the legal pad where she'd been making notes the other day.

"It seems you and the good detective have your own sort of friendship," Frogert said.

Not sure what to make of that comment, Sadie chose to ignore it. Her personal life was none of his business anyway.

"I understand Mr. Bijou visited you here at your store," Frogert continued. "What did he want?"

Sadie wasn't sure why she still found Frogert annoying, but her initial instinct was to hedge about her conversations with Guy. "He was interested in buying an outfit for a lady friend. I suggested one of our new colorful sequined skirts." *Okay, call it more lying than hedging, but why be picky about minor details?*

"Sure he was. What else did he want, Ms. Kramer? Understand I know a little bit about Mr. Bijou's problematic history in New Orleans."

Sadie scribbled the word *problematic* on the pad and underlined it hard three times. "He found out I was the person who discovered Roberta's body, and he suggested her death might have been a copycat of some ghost story he told me."

"Oh?" Froggy seemed surprised that Sadie had offered up so much information, but she suddenly didn't see why she shouldn't. It wasn't Froggy's fault he annoyed her.

"How did Bijou learn you discovered the body?" Now it was Froggy who looked annoyed. "We haven't released that information to the public, not your name or anything about the scene."

From her pillow, Coco opened one eye and gazed at Sadie as if she were asking that question too. *Whose side are you on?* Sadie scratched behind Coco's left ear. "Well, as you might imagine, I wasn't completely myself, so I let my guard down. I thought the young man who approached me just as I was leaving was one of your detectives. He got my name before I realized he was a reporter. He wrote about me on his news site."

"Keith Cross." Frogert muttered the name under his breath almost as if he were cursing.

"You know him?"

"Everyone on the force knows him. He turned up at the murder scene, and I turned him away. Too bad he got to you first."

"Yes, well, Guy seems harmless to me, just a bit desperate to prove his paranormal investigations are legitimate. If I hadn't been careless and given that reporter my name, Guy never would have contacted me."

Frogert tapped his pen against the notebook. "This man may not be as harmless as you think. Someone lost her life on the set during the filming of one of his television episodes. A crew member later claimed Bijou often faked the results of the events on his show."

"Detective, I can't believe Guy would have done something with malice in his heart either at home or here. His beliefs in the paranormal seem genuine. I think he's only trying to help people who believe as he does." *Or convince them to believe? Or simply get the show's ratings up?* Sadie hushed her own thoughts.

Frogert placed one hand on the counter again. "Try telling

that to the woman who was killed," he said, as seriously as she'd ever heard him say anything.

"What exactly happened?"

"You can find details online, but the gist of the story is that, while filming one of his investigations, a stunt Bijou planned backfired, and an object that a supposed poltergeist tossed across a room hit one of his clients in the head, killing her instantly. Bijou claimed the woman's death resembled a legend linked to the house where he and his crew were filming the episode. The producer paused filming while the police, including your friend Broussard, investigated."

Sadie tilted her head to the side, eying the detective curiously. "So let me guess where this is heading. You believe Guy may be here to use that chandelier legend to somehow prove his discoveries are real."

Frogert nodded. "It's possible. It's the type of story he chases after. I suggest you stay away from him, Ms. Kramer, or you may get hurt."

"I'll take that under advisement." Sadie smiled. She loved those television lawyer quips.

"I trust you haven't seen him again?"

Rather than admitting she had, indeed, just seen him at the Wainwright mansion that morning, Sadie simply shook her head. *One non-hedge deserves another?*

"If he approaches you again, please call me," Frogert said as he turned to leave. "Guy Bijou may be dangerous."

TEN

Charlotte was in the back garden, speaking with a trio of gardeners, when Sadie returned to the mansion. At least a dozen flats of bright flowers lay on the ground nearby.

"Coco and I are back!" Sadie said.

"Oh, I knew you'd return. I'm just on edge since we have so little time and no access to the mansion itself. Maggie is doing all she can to help, but she's got foundation business to manage too, and I can't put much more on her shoulders," Charlotte said.

"This has been a tough week for all of you."

Charlotte nodded. "Definitely, including for Maggie. Mother is—was—on the foundation's board of directors. They worked closely together."

"Your mother must have been fond of her," Sadie said, not entirely sure that was the case.

"Yes, she's like part of the family." Charlotte began separating decorations on a wrought iron table, spiders from pumpkins, cobwebs from miniature broomsticks. "I don't think she's even had time to process the fact that Mother is dead. Neither have I, for that matter."

"It takes time," Sadie offered. "And we all grieve in different ways."

"So true," Charlotte said. She lifted a small skeleton by a string attached to its skull and let it dangle for a moment.

"Let's keep going, shall we?" She handed the decoration to Sadie and pointed to a branch in a nearby tree.

"Got it," Sadie said, turning to the task.

"Mother wasn't easy," Charlotte said as she positioned a black bat in a different tree. "She expected Cooper and me to be a certain way, you know? She wanted him to follow in Dad's footsteps, to be an international mogul or whatever Dad is."

"And what did she want from you?"

"What she couldn't get. She wanted me to be stalwart and beautiful. She said I was more anxious than stalwart, and as you can see, I'm anything but beautiful."

Sadie looked into Charlotte's lovely face so much like her mother's, but it held a softness or maybe a kindness Sadie didn't recall seeing in Roberta. Each time she'd visited Flair, she'd demand that Amber *serve* her as if Amber were a lady's maid.

"I think you're quite lovely," Sadie said.

"Oh, thank you." Charlotte lifted a small tombstone off the table of decorations and traced the R.I.P. carved into the cardboard. "I knew I couldn't be beautiful in the way Mother was beautiful, so I tried to be, you know, internally beautiful. I got a degree in social work, you see. That's what I do. I help people who aren't as privileged as I've been."

"You're a good girl," Sadie said.

"Don't call me that, please." Charlotte turned away and cupped her left cheek as if she were caressing someone else's face. "Mother always told me I was a good girl but not pretty enough or charismatic enough to take her place." She shook her head as if to clear it. "Not that I ever *wanted* to take her place. But now…"

Sadie felt a pang of longing to heal the thing in Charlotte

that Roberta had damaged. "Well," she said, "I think you're marvelous on your own."

"She ruined Cooper, you know." Charlotte picked up a length of black yarn and wound it around her index finger. "He wanted to study art. And then, because he thought it would please her more, he switched his major to construction engineering. But she just wanted him to focus on making money, so she bullied him into switching his major to business management. He even ended up getting an MBA, just for Mother. After he got out of school, he didn't have the heart for that kind of work. He said it made his brain hurt. All Cooper wanted to do was flip houses and spend time with pretty girls on beaches. That's why he stayed in Southern California until recently so he could avoid Mother's disapproval."

"But something changed, right?" Sadie thought back to the brief conversation she'd had with Cooper when she met him on the mansion steps. "He told me he and your mother were getting along better."

"Yeah. I guess so, though the tension started all over again when he explained that his big plan for making boatloads of money involved selling off a portion of the Wainwright property to a developer. I heard them discussing it. She said the foundation board would never agree to it and that such a sale would only happen 'Over my dead body.'"

"And how did Cooper react to that?"

"He laughed at her. He said the mansion was never really hers, and he reminded her that she married into it. He said if he could get Dad to agree to the sale, everyone on the board would back him up." Charlotte unwound the yarn and dropped it into the carton of decorations.

"How long ago was this?" Sadie asked.

"Well, Cooper has been back for about three months now.

As far as I know, the topic hasn't come up in several weeks. I do love my brother, Sadie. But I always remembered him being a little bit lazy, and he's always looking for the easy way out."

"What did your father think about selling the property to a developer?" Sadie asked as she plucked a witch's broom from the table.

"I really don't know. I never heard him discuss it with either Mother *or* Cooper. But I think he would have done whatever Mother wanted. He's that kind of husband."

The sound of shuffling footsteps approached, and Sadie and Charlotte both turned to see who had joined them.

"Did someone lose this?" A man in his late sixties or perhaps early seventies held a squirming Coco. He reminded Sadie a bit of Robert Redford, his face handsome but wrinkled.

"Thank you for catching her!" Sadie said as she reached for Coco. "I didn't even see her climb out of my bag!" She whispered a mild but loving reprimand to the ball of fur in her arms.

"Not a problem." He turned toward Charlotte. "I'm sorry we have to wait to set up the big decorations inside like the witches' cauldrons, but I can't get into the ballroom until the police give me the go-ahead." He flinched a little when he said the word *police*.

"I understand, of course," Charlotte said. "We'll just have to do as much as possible on other parts of the property and then rush on the ballroom and other indoor areas as soon as we're allowed." She placed a hand on the man's upper arm affectionately. "How *are* you, Dwight?"

"I'm all right. I wish I hadn't taken that day off. If I'd been here, maybe your mother would still be with us."

"It's not your fault! Please don't feel guilty." Sadie thought

Charlotte looked distraught at the thought that Dwight might blame himself.

"Well, the work on the Spooktacular is keeping my mind off things, so thank you for that."

"No, thank *you*. I would have understood completely if you and Barb had decided you couldn't face the event this year. Cooper is furious with me for going ahead with it."

Sadie was trying to determine Dwight's role in the world of the Wainwright mansion without interrupting this personal moment.

Charlotte glanced at Sadie, who was still holding Coco against her chest. "Dwight is the estate's caretaker. He's the man who's been keeping the Wainwright mansion glistening and in good repair for my entire life. He knows as much about this place as the original builders did."

Sadie bobbed her head since her arms were full of Yorkie, so she couldn't shake hands. "Sadie Kramer," she said. "And this is Coco."

"Dwight Schmidt. It's nice to meet you. Both of you."

"Sadie is helping me with the preparations. She'd been planning to help Mother before…" Charlotte trailed off.

"It's good of you to help our Charlotte," Dwight said.

"I'm happy to do it." Sadie reached into her tote bag and pulled out Coco's leash, clipped it to the dog's collar, and let her down. Coco approached Dwight and sniffed his boots for a little longer than was necessary. Then she sneezed.

Dwight stared down at the little dog, then looked back up at Sadie. "I was quite fond of Roberta. And, yes, she asked me to call her Roberta, though in the old days that wouldn't have been right. I'm going to miss her and her lavish affairs. And her generosity. Though maybe you'll be taking over now, Charlotte."

"I have a job, Dwight," Charlotte said quietly.

"You do, my dear, but jobs can be quit."

"Couldn't Cooper take over?" Sadie asked.

Dwight and Charlotte both laughed, though Sadie felt the laughter was tinged with sadness. "Cooper doesn't have enough anxiety to make a go at filling his mother's shoes. But he is good at some things," Dwight said. "He loves houses as much as his father does and as much as I do. All the Wainwrights love old houses, don't you, Charlotte? Charlotte once told me that one of her favorite Instagram accounts is called For the Love of Old Houses."

Charlotte rolled her eyes.

"Now and then, I give all the Wainwrights lessons in some of the more unique features of the mansion."

Sadie knew that large houses often had secrets that more modern owners didn't discover for years if at all. "What sorts of features?"

"Oh, things like how to open the staircase at the back of the kitchen. You have to knock on it just so." Dwight mimed knocking twice with his large, swollen knuckle. "And there's a trick to making the old dumbwaiter that goes from the kitchen to the master bedroom function without jerking. Sometimes we host guests, and they like the authentic feel of having breakfast arrive on a tray sent up via dumbwaiter."

"You might as well tell her about the chandelier, Dwight," Charlotte said.

"Oh yes! The chandelier." His handsome face grew solemn. "The chandelier. Several months ago, before Cooper came home permanently, he was visiting, and he told me about this astonishing house he was flipping that had a damaged chandelier. He wanted to replace it himself. He said it had a mechanism he'd never seen before, and he couldn't simply climb on a ladder to take it down and repair it. It had some kind of automatic winch. So I offered to show him the mechanism of our ballroom's chandelier."

Sadie gulped. "You did?"

"I did. I gave a lesson to Cooper, his father, and Charlotte here." He gazed at Charlotte fondly. "You were all as giddy as little children at a carnival the way you flicked the switch behind the panel."

"It was really cool, almost as cool as the dumbwaiter," Charlotte said. Sadie wondered if either of them understood the implications of what they were telling her.

"Dwight, do you happen to know if Cooper and that other man are still here? I want to make sure Cooper doesn't let some stranger wander around without supervision, and he just might let him," Charlotte said. "What was his name, Sadie? The ghost investigator guy?"

"Guy Bijou."

Dwight blinked. "*The* Guy Bijou?"

"You know him too?" Sadie said. She was suddenly convinced that only men watched shows about paranormal activity.

"Yes, well, I don't *know* him," Dwight said. He looked down at Coco, who had curled up on top of one of his boots. "I used to watch his show. Found it rather ridiculous to be honest. What is he doing here?"

Sadie and Charlotte exchanged a look. Sadie decided to take on the question. "He seems to think Roberta's death might have been related to a legend he told me about something terrible that happened in the mansion many years ago, well before any of us were born. I'm not sure what he expects from everyone, but it's possible he wants to do an episode about the connection between that story and Roberta's death."

Sadie watched a muscle in Dwight's jaw twitch.

"I hope Cooper sent him packing," he said.

"Not at all," Charlotte said. "In fact, he offered him a beer." She and Sadie both looked back at the area with the cooler. Both chairs were empty. "Did you notice if they were walking around anywhere?"

"I think the three of us are the only ones here right now. I didn't notice Cooper's car out front anymore, so I'm guessing he, at least, is gone." Dwight looked at Sadie. "Is Guy the kind of person who would snoop on his own?"

Of course he is. "I don't know," Sadie said. "I only just met the man myself."

"Well, I'll let you get back to your decorations. I think I'll go search the grounds to make sure we don't have a trespasser."

ELEVEN

Sadie curled up in her living room armchair and looked out the window at the city lights, a glass of chardonnay next to her on the end table. Coco wrestled with her plush lobster by the sofa. A murder mystery lay open in Sadie's lap, but she wasn't reading. Try as she might to get her mind off the Wainwright situation, she kept thinking about who might have wanted Roberta dead and why. Was Roberta in the way of something someone wanted? Did she have any enemies? She didn't seem like the kind of person who would have enemies beyond people who might have been envious or maybe found her a little blunt. Did her murder have anything to do with the Wainwright Foundation? Had someone tried to embezzle funds and Roberta found out? Did her death have something to do with the mansion? And—crazy as it sounded—did some kind of supernatural spirit cause Roberta's death?

"Stop right there," she said to herself. "There are no such things as ghosts, goblins, or spirits. Something—no, some*one*—human murdered Roberta." She wished she had that legal pad from the store where she'd been scrawling notes, words, and ideas. Nothing on the pad made sense or connected, but something about the process of putting pencil to paper helped her think. She understood more why Froggy tapped his pen against his notebook and why Keith Cross's first action upon learning her name was to pull out *his* notebook. She sighed, stood up, and walked to her small home desk, where her personal laptop rested. She found a small spiral-bound notebook in a drawer, pulled a pencil out of the pencil holder, and returned to her chair. Just as she was about to scratch down the first word, which was going to be *mask*, her cell phone buzzed.

Broussard! she thought as she reached for the phone. But one glance at the number told her it wasn't him. "Hello?"

"Sadie, this is Charlotte Wainwright. Sorry to bother you so late in the evening."

Sadie glanced at her watch. It was nearly ten o'clock. She hadn't realized so much time had gone by since she'd arrived home. "It's fine. I tend to be a night owl. What can I do for you?"

Charlotte laughed, and Sadie imagined she heard a little embarrassment in the voice that sounded so much like Roberta's. "I do always seem to be asking you for something, don't I?"

"It's all right. You're going through something huge. How are preparations progressing for the Spooktacular?"

"I don't even know where to start," Charlotte said. "That's why I'm calling you, actually. I've only just gotten home. I worked well past dark. After you left, I started making lists of what we still needed to do, and while Maggie can help me with some of it, as I told you, she has to deal with her day job and all the calls she's getting related to Mother's... you know. Dwight has offered to deal with some of the larger spooky elements, especially once we get into the ballroom. But honestly, I'm panicking. Even with the work crew we hired, there's too much to do and too little time." Sadie could hear Charlotte take a deep breath. "Is there any chance you'd be able to help with a few more things?"

Sadie paused, wondering how she would juggle store tasks with helping set up the event. She also had a strong suspicion that "a few more things" might just turn out to be more than a few more things. But Amber was more than capable of running Flair, and the week before Halloween was hardly like the week before Christmas. Besides, helping Charlotte might lend itself to finding out what really happened to Roberta. "Sure," she said. "I'll be glad to help. Just tell me what you need."

"Thank you! Oh, I thought I should let you know that Guy person turned up again this evening, and Dwight caught him trying to sneak into the mansion despite the police tape. The door was locked, thank goodness. He seems to be a bit of a menace, that one," Charlotte said.

Sadie thought "menace" might be an exaggeration. She sensed in Guy a kindred spirit with a curiosity that matched her own, though his methods of acquiring information and his reasons for wanting that information were far different from hers. "If I see him again, maybe I'll have a word with him. I don't think he means to intrude or frighten you. He's just determined."

"It *would* be great if you could speak to him, Sadie, thank you. And I'll make a little list for you tonight. Maybe you could pick it up tomorrow at the Wainwright Foundation office?"

"That sounds fine," Sadie said. "I have errands to run tomorrow anyway. I'll stop by sometime in the morning."

"Excellent. I'll be there early. That is such a relief to me!"

Sadie ended the call, set her phone down, and looked over at the sleeping Yorkie cuddled up with the stuffed red lobster. "Well, Coco, I guess we'll just see if Charlotte's *little* list of a *few* more things turns out to give new meaning to the words *little* and *few*."

TWELVE

S adie rose early in the morning to get a head start on the day. She needed to pick up some extra plastic garment bags from the twenty-four-hour big box store since Flair was running low. Sales had been better than she'd anticipated, so she hadn't ordered enough, and the next shipment wouldn't arrive for a week or so. She also needed to go to the dry cleaners to pick up a lovely red silk dress she thought might work as an impromptu costume for the Spooktacular. And she'd promised Charlotte she'd stop by for the list of volunteer tasks.

After a cup of coffee with her favorite french vanilla creamer, she decided she felt like wearing something that reminded her of the bright light outside, so she chose a soft yellow tunic with a high neck and a pair of cream-colored slacks. She was delighted to find that a recently acquired pair of black-and-white-striped flats and clip-on onyx earrings completed the outfit to her satisfaction. Bearing a strange resemblance to a bumble bee, she was ready to face the day.

She ate an English muffin with just the smallest smear of strawberry jam, fed Coco her breakfast, and patted a bit of blush onto her cheeks before she gathered Coco and the tote and headed down to her car.

Her first stop was Nikko's, her favorite dry cleaners. She'd been bringing her clothes, quilts, jackets, and coats to Nikko for years. He'd become a kind of friend after all this time, though she sometimes still had trouble understanding him because of his thick Greek accent that grew even thicker when he was excited. He was a good sort of person to encounter first thing in the morning. Nikko was one of the most joyful people Sadie had ever met.

She parked, tucked Coco into her tote, and entered the shop. Dozens and dozens of dresses, suits, and coats hung from the moving racks behind the large, clean counter. Nikko stood with his arms folded, a huge smile on his face. "Sadie, Sadie! I knew I'd get to see your beautiful self this morning!"

Sadie smiled in return. "You're the beautiful one, Nikko." Although Nikko's thick hair was completely white, his bushy mustache was nearly black and draped over his upper lip like a fringe. Sadie stifled a chuckle when she compared this glorious bit of facial hair to Froggy's sparse attempt.

He laughed. "You are here for your red dress? You will be 'the lady in red' on a dance floor soon?"

"Something like that."

Nikko leaned over the counter a bit and gestured toward Sadie's tote. "And how is our princess this morning?"

"She's perfect as always."

"I think I have a little something here for her." Nikko always had a little something for Coco. He pulled a tiny treat out of a cup he kept underneath the counter. Coco popped up, paws on the tote's edge, and opened her tiny mouth. Sadie lifted Coco onto the counter and put the tote on the floor. Nikko let the pup take the biscuit from the palm of his hand.

"Give me just one moment," Nikko said, and he vanished into the forest of plastic bags and quickly reemerged. "Here you are."

Sadie hung the dress on a cart near the counter so she

could dig into her tote for her wallet. She slid her credit card through the reader, and Nikko handed her the receipt. "Nikko, would it be possible for me to purchase some extra garment bags from you? I have a box full coming in soon, but we're nearly out, and we expect some decent sales for the rest of the week and through the weekend," she said and pulled a ten-dollar bill from her wallet.

"You are most welcome to some bags, but purchasing is not necessary. They are yours." Nikko handed Sadie a bagful of bags.

"Oh, thank you so much! Until next time, my friend," she said as she scooped Coco back into the tote and plucked the dress off the rack.

She juggled the dress, the bag of bags, and Coco into the car and drove to the Wainwright Foundation's headquarters, which was a few blocks to the west of the mansion itself on a quiet cul-de-sac in a residential neighborhood. It was based in a building that used to be a boarding house back in the 1950s. Like the Wainwright mansion, it was built in the late 1800s. Sadie found it far more charming than the mansion, but she was more inclined to prefer her luxury structures on a more scaled-down size. The narrow little house had a turret, which she recalled Roberta once saying was her office. She suspected that was where she would find Charlotte.

With the tote bag strap secured on her shoulder, Sadie hauled herself up the steps that curled around in an elegant spiral until she reached the top floor. The office door was open, and the sound of a printer spilled out onto the landing.

"Hello?" Sadie called quietly as she walked into the office.

Charlotte sat behind the mahogany pedestal desk, staring at a sheet of paper in front of her. Her face was pale, and her hands were clenched into fists on either side of what looked to Sadie like a handwritten letter.

"Charlotte? Are you all right?"

Charlotte looked up. "Ms. Kramer? Oh, I'm so glad you're here."

Sadie ventured farther into the room, which was full of morning light. "Please call me Sadie. I just wanted to pick up that list of things that you need me to help with. And to see how you're doing, of course."

"How I'm doing? I hardly know." Charlotte stood up, still staring at the paper on the desk.

"It must be difficult for you to take your mother's place so soon," Sadie said.

"I'm just trying to fill her shoes for the Spooktacular for now."

Sadie waited for a hint or gesture or something to let her know whether Charlotte meant for her to stay or wanted her to leave her in peace, but Charlotte simply remained behind the desk, looking down at the letter. Sadie was quite certain by now that it was not the list of tasks she'd planned to pick up.

"Well, if you need anything, you have my numbers. I can always make time of course. Now that you've decided the event is to go on as planned, I know you have a lot to do. Just call me whenever you want."

Just as Sadie turned to leave, Charlotte spoke. "Sadie, I found something rather upsetting, and I'm not sure what to do with it. I know we don't know each other well, but you were my mother's friend, and you may be able to advise me."

A customer is not a friend, Sadie thought, but then felt that to be ungenerous. Maybe Charlotte needed someone who, at least because of her own age, could fill what was now a maternal void.

Charlotte pinched a corner of the letter between her thumb

and forefinger and handed it to Sadie. "I'm not sure this is the right thing to do. I'm not even sure I should have read this, but I did. It's just so upsetting, and I feel overwhelmed. What should I do with this? What do you think?" Sadie sat in the straight-backed chair with a cushion consisting of a beautiful floral pattern in front of the desk, and Charlotte, too, sat down. She watched as Sadie glanced at the letter and then read it thoroughly. It was undated.

Dearest Maggie,

This letter is one of the hardest things I've ever had to write. You are a beautiful, vibrant woman, and I care for you deeply. But I cannot proceed with a relationship with you. I cannot leave Roberta for you. She's been my partner in business, parenting, and life for forty years. She's a good woman, and she doesn't deserve my betrayal.

But I do confess that my feelings for you are strong, and if I weren't committed to this marriage I chose so many years ago when I was a young man, I would want to have you by my side. I meant the vows I made when I said, "Till death do us part."

I hope we can put this moment behind us and that you'll continue to serve as the Wainwright Foundation's executive director. We've worked together for a long, long time, you, Roberta, and I. Let's not let our emotions affect the good work we've all been doing for our community.

Fondly,
Seymour

Sadie let the letter fall into her lap and looked up at Charlotte, whose dark gray eyes so similar to her brother's seemed filled with pain. "Well. This is quite the note. How did you come across it?"

Charlotte took a deep breath. "I went to Maggie's office early this morning, looking for a list of vendors she told me she had. She doesn't usually come in until nine or ten, and she called to say she'd be even later today. I needed the list to confirm orders we placed for the Spooktacular. I'm afraid I sorted through things on her desk, looking for the list. When I didn't find it, I searched through the desk drawers and found that instead." She pointed at the paper in Sadie's lap. "I couldn't help myself when I saw my father's handwriting. I had to read it. I feel awful about invading Maggie's privacy, but, Sadie, what does this mean? Is my father having an affair with Maggie Barton?"

Sadie shook her head and handed the letter back to Charlotte. "I don't know. It doesn't specifically say so. But I completely understand why you're so upset. Perhaps you should ask your father?"

"Or Maggie. Maybe I should ask Maggie." Charlotte stood again and seemed to be about to leave the office. She looked frantic. *A Wainwright in the wild*, Sadie thought. Coco let out a yip from deep inside the tote bag.

"Or maybe you should take another breath," Sadie suggested. "Confronting Maggie might upset you even more. Also, didn't you say Maggie is coming in late today?" Sadie wasn't looking forward to the possibility of hysterics from either woman, though what she'd seen of Maggie the other day indicated she was fairly calm and focused.

"She might be here by now. Do you think... Oh no." Her voice dropped to a whisper, and her eyes grew wide. "Do you think Maggie might have… *hurt* Mother?"

Sadie sighed. There was no way to answer a question like that. "I think you should take this letter to Detective Frogert before jumping to conclusions. Let the police do their job."

Charlotte took a step back. "I… I don't think I can face him. I don't think I can talk about anything that might be related to what happened to my mother. Would you do it for me, Sadie? I'd be so grateful."

Again, Sadie heard Roberta in Charlotte's voice, and she felt a sudden pang of grief. Even though she hadn't known Roberta Wainwright well, she had known her for a while. Her death was causing a great deal of pain. She knew it would probably be better for Charlotte to take Froggy the letter, easier to explain how it came into her possession, but Sadie decided doing this for Charlotte was the kind and right thing to do. "I will. But the detective will probably need to talk to you about this at some point."

Charlotte linked her fingers as if in prayer and pressed them against her belly. "I will talk to him. I will. I just can't do it now. Thank you so, so much. I'm eternally grateful." Charlotte then came forward and hugged Sadie briefly.

* * *

Sadie tucked the folded letter into a side pocket of her tote bag along with the to-do list, said goodbye to Charlotte, who looked exhausted and stricken, and made her way down the spiral staircase to the second floor. She wasn't sure where Maggie's office might be, so she walked down the hallway, trying to guess which room might be hers. The third door on the right was open, so Sadie and Coco stepped over the threshold for a moment. The office was empty.

A large glass-topped desk that contrasted oddly with the old-fashioned dark wood paneling and the fancy wainscoting was littered with folders and papers. In a gold-framed photograph, what appeared to be a teenaged Maggie stood next to a beaming, balding man in a brown suit. *Her father?* A pen lay on top of a notebook, the page open to a to-do list. Sadie glanced toward the door and then turned the notebook toward her.

- *Call attorneys*
- Check with C about prop dev
- Go to costume store
- Review budget
- Discuss plans for distributing funds raised during the Spooktacular
- *Call Seymour!!*

Sadie replaced the notebook where she'd found it and let herself out of the building. Annoying though she found Detective Frogert, she was going to have to visit him for Charlotte's sake. And for Roberta's. Once Sadie had Coco settled, she pulled Froggy's business card out of her bag and dialed.

"Frogert!" the detective growled into the phone.

"It's Sadie Kramer, Detective. I was wondering if I could see you this morning? It's about Roberta Wainwright's murder."

"Still snooping around, Ms. Kramer?"

Sadie rolled her eyes. Coco tilted her head to one side. "I know. I know," she mouthed to her wee companion. "I'm not snooping, Detective. Charlotte Wainwright asked me to bring you something that may be helpful to your investigation."

"And what is this 'something,' hmm? And why can't she

bring it to me herself?" Froggy sounded crankier than usual.

"She's feeling particularly upset today for a variety of reasons. I agreed to help her out with this. She promised me she'd be happy to talk to you later if you need her to." Sadie imagined she could hear Froggy tapping his pen against his mustache.

"Fine. I guess I'll take whatever this is however I can get it."

"I can be at the precinct in just a few minutes," Sadie said.

"Um, no, I was just about to go out to pick up something to eat. The wife is out of town, and I'm afraid I'm much better at solving cases than I am at feeding myself."

Sadie couldn't help the short, sharp laugh that slipped out. "All right, Detective. Name the place, and I'll be there."

"I'll be at the Java Sun Café. And Ms. Kramer?"

"Yes, Detective?"

"You'd better not try to milk me for information about Roberta Wainwright's murder."

"*Moi*? Though if I can do anything to help…"

Froggy snorted and hung up the phone.

THIRTEEN

Sadie pulled into the small parking lot of the Java Sun Café, performed the ritual of tucking Coco safely into the tote bag, and put Seymour's letter into the pocket of her jacket so she wouldn't have to hunt around for it.

The bell on the door jingled as she pushed it open, and warmth and a rush of scents—especially coffee and cinnamon—enveloped her. She didn't yet see Froggy. Deciding she deserved a treat after the drama at the foundation headquarters, she ordered a chocolate croissant and a latte, found a small table near the front window, and sat herself down with her tote bag on her lap to wait for her order. She had a good view of the people coming and going, so she knew she wouldn't miss the detective's arrival.

Sadie loved to people watch. She liked to describe what she saw to Coco, though this act sometimes drew stares from people who thought she was either talking to herself or talking to a tote bag. "Coco," she whispered, "you should see the marvelous hat on this woman. She's wrapped a fuchsia scarf around the crown, and the tail of the scarf blows out behind her like a wedding veil." A gaunt man in a black suit scissored his way through a crowd of young girls, some with hands linked, who followed a tall, broad-shouldered woman who must have been a teacher or chaperone.

The front door's bell jingled again, and Detective Frogert entered the café. He wore a light gray trench coat over his suit, and the wrinkles in the fabric reminded Sadie of an elephant's leg. He looked around the café until he spotted her, waved, and stood in line to place his order.

Sadie pulled the letter out of her jacket pocket and smoothed it open on the table in front of her, careful to avoid a damp spot. She skimmed through it again, trying to read between the lines. Was Seymour having an affair with Maggie? Or was he merely tempted? The wording was vague enough that either scenario could be the case.

Froggy set down his to-go bag and a large coffee and sat across from Sadie just as a young woman brought Sadie her croissant and latte.

Froggy took off the lid on his coffee, sipped, then winced. "Hot." He replaced the lid. "Now. What's this 'something' you want to show me that Ms. Wainwright was too broken up to bring me herself?"

Sadie drank some of her latte, which was in a ceramic mug rather than a to-go cup. "Charlotte found this in Maggie Barton's desk at the foundation headquarters." She handed him the paper. "It appears to be a sort of love letter from Seymour Wainwright to Maggie."

As he read the letter quickly, his eyebrows rose higher and higher. He didn't say anything, looked up at Sadie, then read the note again.

"What do you think?" Sadie finally asked, anxious to hear Froggy's response.

"What do I think? I think I need more information about Ms. Barton's activities the day Mrs. Wainwright was killed." He folded the letter and placed it into his shirt pocket. Sadie eyed the pocket longingly. Maybe she should have stopped at Flair to make a copy. "How well do you know Ms. Barton?" Froggy asked.

"Not well at all. I only met her the other day at the mansion where she was helping Charlotte with some things related to the Spooktacular event coming up this weekend. Maggie was in quite a hurry. I believe she had an interview with you at the foundation headquarters."

Froggy stood, patted the letter in his pocket, and gathered his coffee and bag of food. "Well, she's about to have another interview with me. Thank you for this, Ms. Kramer." The detective turned to leave, but Sadie reached out a hand as if to stop him.

"Detective Frogert, do you know exactly *how* Roberta died?"

"You know I can't tell you that, Ms. Kramer. You promised not to ply me for information."

"I did no such thing," Sadie said. "You simply asked me not to. That's not the same thing as me agreeing."

Frogert made a sort of grunting sound, seemingly unwilling to concede the distinction.

"I mostly wanted to make sure the dear woman didn't suffer." Sadie cupped her mug between her hands.

Froggy seemed to consider whether to answer or not. "All right, I suppose you've earned a little information, but don't go blabbing this around. The autopsy showed Mrs. Wainwright died of blunt-force trauma to the head."

Sadie shuddered. That phrase was so, well, blunt.

"We're fairly certain she didn't suffer. Most likely she died instantly. That's all I can tell you."

"Well, that's good to hear that she didn't suffer. But I still wonder how it happened. Was it the chandelier?" She thought back to the thud she'd heard when she was searching the mansion for Roberta. No. The thud came before the sound of shattering glass. "Maybe you could just tell me what the killer used...?" Sadie knew she was pressing, but it went against her nature to rein in her curiosity.

"That's enough for now, Ms. Kramer. Thank you for bringing me this letter."

"You're welcome, Detective. Do let me know if there's any other way I can help."

Froggy glowered for a moment, shook his head, and left the café.

"Well, look at that, Coco," Sadie whispered into her tote bag. "Froggy finally gave us a crumb of a detail." She broke off a bite of her croissant and closed her eyes as she tasted a delicious rush of dark chocolate and buttery pastry. When she opened them again, she was startled to see a familiar figure strolling from the café register toward a nearby table.

Cooper Wainwright didn't notice her, and she chose not to call attention to herself. She wondered if Charlotte had called to tell him about the note her father had written to Maggie. He didn't look particularly upset. *Most people don't wear their emotions on their faces when they're out in public*, Sadie thought. After the argument she witnessed between the siblings at the mansion, she wasn't sure how willing Charlotte would be to share anything with her brother.

Cooper pulled a folder from a laptop case and set the case on the floor between his feet. He flipped the folder open and ran his index finger down what she guessed was a column on a sheet of paper. *Numbers?* Sadie thought.

A moment later, a man joined Cooper, and Sadie wished she had a book, a large menu, or newspaper to hide behind. The reporter, Keith Cross, was not someone Sadie wanted to see.

"Nice to see you, Keith," Cooper stood and shook the reporter's hand.

"Same," Cross said. "How are you holding up, man?"

One of the young baristas, a girl with a high, blond ponytail, placed a plate in front of Cooper. "The brunch special, spinach quiche and a fruit cup."

"Thanks, honey," Cooper said as he turned back to Keith. "I'm dealing just fine. I think the only way to get through something as traumatic as this is to stay busy. And it's especially important to look forward."

"And that looking forward is why you called me?" Cross glanced around the café and lowered his voice slightly. Sadie wished she were wearing something more drab, but like Cooper, the reporter didn't see her. "Are you really going through with the sale? I thought your mother was totally against it."

Cooper slid the open folder to Keith. "When I showed her these figures, she started to change her mind. If she hadn't died, I'm sure I could have convinced her to do the right thing."

Keith looked over whatever was in the folder. "The last time I interviewed her about the Spooktacular and brought up the possibility of selling off the orchard, she didn't seem particularly enthusiastic," he said. "In fact, she seemed convinced that developing that land would hurt the work the Wainwright Foundation does."

Cooper dug his fork into his quiche, took a bite, chewed for a moment, and then swallowed. "And when did you last speak to her?"

"The day before she died. Why are telling me all this anyway? Why are you showing me these numbers? Isn't this something you should keep between you and the buyer for now?"

Cooper pointed his fork at Keith. "Don't you want a scoop? I want to get this information out to the public so the executive director of the foundation and the rest of the board will feel obliged to approve the sale."

Keith shoved the folder back toward Cooper. "Seems a bit Machiavellian, Cooper. And I'm a journalist, not a press release writer. You need to call a different department if you're looking for publicity."

"Fine," Cooper said. "Then I'll find someone else to give this exclusive to. Your loss."

Keith pushed back his chair and stood. "I'm really sorry about what happened to your mother. Give my condolences to your sister and father."

"Sure!" Cooper said as he took the paperwork back, retrieved his laptop case from between his feet, and slipped the folder inside, then returned to his meal as his phone rang. The ringtone, the first bars of Pink Floyd's "Money," played too loudly. He ate while he listened to whoever was on the other side of the call. "Yeah, yeah, I'm working on it," he said. He kept the phone pressed to his ear while he dug his fork into the quiche.

Sadie bent her head toward her tote and whispered, "What an interesting conversation, don't you think, Coco?"

"Ms. Kramer?"

When she raised her head, Keith Cross was standing opposite her. He took the seat Froggy had vacated just a little while ago.

"Have you been here long?" he asked. He glanced at the tote in her lap but said nothing. It was a reaction Sadie was used to. Few people asked why she talked to her bag. Which, of course, was a good thing.

"A little while," she said. "I was meeting with a… friend, but he had to leave, and I decided to stay for a bit to enjoy this lovely latte and a croissant." Sadie glanced toward Cooper, who was still on the phone and hadn't noticed her or that the reporter had stopped to talk to her. She looked at Keith and waited to see what he wanted. She was beginning to feel overwhelmed and somewhat desperate to get to Flair where she could call Froggy again to tell him what she'd just overheard. Or maybe Broussard. Or maybe she would just hide in her office.

"Would you mind if I asked you some questions about what you saw the day you found Roberta Wainwright's body?" Keith pulled his ubiquitous notebook and pen out of his jacket pocket and clicked the pen three times. "Can you tell me anything at all?"

"I really can't," Sadie said. "I'm not comfortable talking about it. You could try asking at the police station."

"Already tried that," Keith said. "Funny how they never want to give out inside information. It would make my job so much easier."

Sadie looked down at the half-eaten croissant, wondering if it would be impolite to take a bite in front of the reporter. She decided to wait. As she wrapped it in a napkin to save for later, it occurred to her that an opportunity had just presented itself, especially with Cooper focused on food and phone calls. "I couldn't help overhearing your discussion with Cooper Wainwright, something about a sale?"

"Oh, that." Keith waved his hand dismissively. "Same old story. The Wainwright family has been arguing about selling off a section of the property for several months. It's a double block, you know, very valuable real estate here in San Francisco. One of the last few parcels of that type not developed yet."

"But it's a gorgeous mansion!" Sadie exclaimed. "Those marble steps and entryway, the spacious ballroom. It would be a shame to see it gone."

Keith laughed as he put his notepad and pen away. "That's the point many of the Wainwright Foundation board members and the family are discussing, and it's Cooper's main argument. It wouldn't be gone. The sale would only include the orchard half, not the mansion."

"So the family would keep the mansion and still gain the money from the sale?" Sadie's only experience with real estate was watching Morris's development deals. But it sounded like a reasonable proposal. Then again, high-rise buildings overshadowing the mansion didn't strike her as very appealing. "I heard you say Roberta was against development. Do you know how Seymour and Charlotte feel?"

"I think Charlotte is against, though she tends to duck my attempts to interview her, and I've never actually met her. Seymour could probably be swayed, though I know he loves the mansion itself. I don't see him as caring that much for flowers and trees. Not his style, if you know what I mean."

"I see," Sadie said. She didn't know Seymour well enough to be able to determine whether he was a nature lover, but she suspected that he was more comfortable in board rooms than forests.

"Are you sure I can't get just a few details from you about the crime scene?" Keith prodded. "How about one detail, just one?"

Sadie shook her head and took this as a chance to escape. "I'm sorry I can't help you. And I'm afraid Coco and I are late for work."

"Coco?" Keith asked as Sadie stood and cuddled the tote bag to her chest.

Sadie leaned toward Keith, gesturing to the bag. "Coco is my dog," she whispered. "Shh, I don't think this establishment allows animals."

At the sound of her name, Coco popped her head up out of the tote and barked once. Several heads turned, including that of the person behind the register.

"That's my cue," Sadie said, and she fled the café for the parking lot.

FOURTEEN

As Sadie drove away from the Java Sun Café, a double buzz from her cell phone told her that she had an incoming text. She pulled over to the side of the road, took her phone out of her purse, and smiled at the familiar greeting.

Ms. Kramer
Detective Broussard
How are you doing?

Sadie debated how she should answer this. Sitting on the side of the road wasn't an opportune time to fill Broussard in on her meeting with Charlotte, the revelation of Seymour's love letter and confession, or the chance sighting of Cooper Wainwright and Keith Cross at the café. Not to mention the connections between all of them. She settled on the simplest answer she could come up with.

Fine.

There, Sadie told herself. She reached her right hand over her left shoulder and gave herself a pat on the back for being clever and succinct. A young girl in a passing car waved, as if Sadie's gesture were meant for her. Sadie waved back at the child, then turned her attention back to the phone, not expecting the next text that arrived.

Do you have plans for this evening?

The unexpected question threw Sadie off, and she wasn't

sure how to respond. Perhaps he wanted to set up a time to talk on the phone? Had he discovered something about Guy Bijou since their last conversation? Something that might implicate him in Roberta's murder? The thought made her a little sad. She'd taken a liking to the odd but seemingly nice paranormal investigator.

Just the usual. Hot date, nightclub hopping. Sadie let out a half-giggle, half-cackle sound after sending the text, earning a questioning look from Coco.

Sounds exciting, Broussard sent back, not taking the bait. *In that case, how about the number of a good San Francisco taxi company?*

Sadie caught her breath. Could this mean what she thought it did? Was Broussard flying in from New Orleans?

Does this mean what it sounds like? Sadie fluffed her hair nervously while waiting for an answer. She hadn't seen Broussard since her trip to New Orleans, although they'd developed a solid friendship since then through phone calls and texts. Okay, she admitted it was a little more than friendship, at least she thought it was.

If it sounds like I need a ride from the San Francisco airport tonight, then yes. But I can take a taxi to the hotel.

Absolutely not, Sadie typed back. *What flight? What time?*

United 1552, 9:47 pm. I'm meeting with Frogert in the morning.

About Guy Bijou? It had to be, Sadie thought.

We think there might be a connection between the cases. I need to get to the airport. See you tonight.

I'll be there.

Sadie sent the last text and slipped her phone into a side pocket on her tote bag.

"Well, Coco, what do you think of that? Broussard is

coming to San Francisco." The Yorkie responded with her usual yip, a contribution to the discussion even if not an actual answer to Sadie's question. Not that Sadie expected an answer. She wasn't sure herself what she thought of Broussard's unexpected visit. A light fluttering sensation tickled her chest, immediately followed by self-chastising. How silly of her to feel like a schoolgirl. This was an official police visit, not a romantic rendezvous. Froggy and Broussard had serious detective work to do. Broussard had said so himself that there could be a connection between their two cases.

Calming her nerves, Sadie pulled back onto the road and ran this new information through her mind. She could see how the case involving Guy Bijou's set and Roberta Wainwright's murder were similar. In Broussard's case, which involved the *Ghosts and Goblins* death, from what Froggy had told her, Guy was either attempting to create a reenactment of a ghost or poltergeist legend or he was filming what he claimed was a real and immediate paranormal incident for his show. In each scenario, a woman had died under circumstances involving paranormal legends.

Guy Bijou had been on the scene when the woman in New Orleans had died, since he would obviously be on the set for the filming of any of his shows. But the Wainwright mansion hadn't been set up for shooting one of Guy's episodes. There was no crew, no cameras, no microphones or paranormal tracking equipment. The ballroom was empty except for Roberta's body and the broken chandelier.

The occurrence at the mansion only resembled the other because both were tied to paranormal legends. The fact Guy Bijou happened to be in San Francisco at the time was merely a coincidence. Or was it?

Sadie started for home but out of habit headed for Flair.

She always liked checking in there to see if Amber needed help with anything. And her office computer seemed to be calling her for research purposes. Were Froggy and Broussard onto something? Were there details about the New Orleans case that she wasn't aware of but might be found in the internet? The media had a way of spilling information though not all of it could be trusted. The challenge was separating what was true and what was either exaggerated or simply opinion.

When Sadie arrived at the shop, Amber was in the process of steaming a beige linen dress that she'd retrieved from a dressing room floor. She looked up at Sadie and sighed.

"I wish everyone would be courteous enough to put clothing back on hangers after trying things on," Amber said.

Sadie nodded. "I agree. Fortunately, most of our customers are respectful. There will always be a few who are inconsiderate. In any business, really. Look at Matteo's shop next door. Occasionally someone will try a sample and just drop the paper cup on the floor."

"I've seen that happen," Amber said. "It doesn't make any sense. There's a trash receptacle right next to the sample tray." Amber held the dress up by the hanger and shook it out. "There, much better." She replaced it on a clothing rack with similar dresses and put the steamer away in the back of the shop while Sadie placed Coco on her counter pillow.

"Busy morning?" Sadie asked when Amber returned to the front.

"Not too bad. We had a few sales. Mostly odds and ends that can be used for costumes. Lots of black, a French-style beret, and some items from the vintage rack and shelves, including those cool elbow-length gloves. What's new with you?" Amber pulled a rag and glass cleaner from the shelving under the front counter and started wiping down the glass.

"I've been everywhere today, including the Wainwright Foundation office."

"Oh gosh." Amber stopped wiping the glass down for a minute. "They must all be so upset there. Any new updates on Roberta's... well, you know."

Sadie understood the unfinished sentence. Murder wasn't an easy word to spit out, especially when the victim was someone she knew. "No major developments," Sadie said. She kept her promise to Froggy and didn't share the cause of death. "But I did have an interesting conversation with Charlotte. She found something that might be important."

"What was it?"

"A letter to Maggie, the foundation's executive director."

A customer entered the shop and aimed for a sales rack near the front of the store.

"What kind of letter?" Amber whispered.

Sadie took a piece of scratch paper from a pile next to the register, scribbled the words, *love letter* on it, and slid it in front of Amber, whose eyebrows immediately lifted. Sadie nodded and motioned toward the back of the shop to indicate she'd be in the office while Amber helped the customer.

Firing up her office computer, Sadie took advantage of the time to run a quick search on *Guy's Ghosts and Goblins*. The show's website only had complimentary posts, nothing scandalous. This she expected. However, a few Google searches brought up different stories, ranging from concerns about lack of safety precautions to outright accusations of intent to harm on Guy Bijou's part.

It wasn't long before Sadie heard the sound of the register ringing up a sale, followed by the jangle of the front door's bell as the customer departed. In seconds, Amber was standing in front of Sadie's desk, the office door propped open to be sure they'd hear if another customer entered.

"What kind of love letter?"

"You know," Sadie said. "The kind expressing love for someone?"

Amber shifted her weight from one hip to the other. "Well, that's a good thing, right?"

Sadie shook her head. "Not in this case. Not when Charlotte's father wrote it."

"You mean Roberta's husband? And it was to a different woman?"

Sadie nodded. "To Maggie."

"So Mr. Wainwright was going to leave his wife for another woman, and his daughter finds this out now, right after her mother dies," Amber said. "How sad."

"It's more complicated than that," Sadie said. "The letter told the woman that he was *not* going to leave his wife for her. But it did express his love, and it also noted that they'd be together if not for his sense of 'Till death do us part' duty to stay with Roberta."

"So with Roberta out of the way..." Amber's voice trailed off. "It sounds like this Maggie person had a lot to gain from Roberta's death. I see motive written all over this scenario."

"Perhaps," Sadie said. "We can't jump to conclusions though. Charlotte asked me to turn the letter over to Froggy, which I did. It was the right thing to do."

"Poor Charlotte, finding this out on top of losing her mom."

"Yes. And poor Seymour when his daughter confronts him. I'm sure that won't be a pleasant conversation. Emotions are already running high in that family."

"So, do you think Maggie killed Roberta?"

"I think that's for the police to decide. Speaking of which..." Sadie stood up and began to gather her things and get Coco settled back in the tote. "I need to get home. I'm picking a certain detective up at the airport later."

Amber's face lit up. "Broussard? From New Orleans? Of course it is. You're blushing!"

"I am not." Sadie hoisted her Yorkie-laden bag over her shoulder and touched her face with the back of her hand. It did feel a bit flushed, but she wasn't about to admit it.

The chime of the front door signaled the arrival of two women, regular customers chattering happily as they entered.

"Don't you dare let him leave town without coming in here to introduce himself," Amber said as she started for the front of the store. "I'm dying to meet him."

Sadie laughed. "I'll keep that in mind. Oh, and Amber?"

"Yes?" Amber stuck her head halfway back into the office while watching one of the women hold a sweater up in front of a mirror.

"You might not want to use those exact words when referring to a homicide detective."

FIFTEEN

S adie glanced at the clock and realized it was later than she thought. Coco had overslept. Sadie could almost tell time by Coco's habits. Her regular afternoon nap gave Sadie quiet time to reflect on the day's events while Coco most likely dreamed of an unlimited bowl of treats or an enthusiastic cat chase.

Luckily, Sadie was all set to pick Broussard up at the airport. She'd planned to get on the way before sunset, and there was still time. This would allow just enough twilight for Sadie to catch Van Ness, named after San Francisco's seventh mayor, down to the 101 freeway. She smiled as the random trivia crossed her mind. She knew almost every past San Francisco mayor's name and tenure due to her late husband's real estate dealings with the city. Sadie had helped Morris prepare for important meetings by reciting past mayors' accomplishments.

Nudging Coco gently to wake her up, Sadie headed for her closet while the Yorkie stretched and yawned. She discarded the soft robe she'd been wearing since showering earlier and looked at the outfit she'd picked out to wear to the airport. Convinced she'd chosen well, she slipped on the casual slacks and royal blue sweater with a cowl neckline that was just soft enough to be alluring without looking too overly sweet. She added a peacock brooch and sapphire stud earrings to pick up the sweater's color. Paying extra attention to her hair and makeup, she gathered her jacket, purse, and of course, dog,

DEBORAH GARNER

and headed out.

Sadie left her private garage at the base of her building and aimed for the freeway. Once she reached Hwy 101, she glanced toward the tall buildings on Rincon Hill, one of which was now dubbed "The Leaning Tower of San Francisco" for its unfortunate engineering defects. She continued over to Mission and past Bernal Heights. As always, traffic slowed to a crawl, but Sadie had anticipated this. She followed her plan to take another route, up 280 toward Colma for the view of the lights below and a detour and stop that she'd contemplated since learning that Broussard would be flying in. She would take 380 back down to 101 to continue to the airport.

She hadn't been to Colma for some time, though it had been her habit to visit every month or two for many years after her husband, Morris, had passed away. His grave was one of many—an understatement—in the "City of Souls," an unusual town with more residents dead than alive.

Before he died, Morris had warned Sadie about remarrying, given their wealth. He wanted to be sure she wouldn't want for anything after he was gone. Yet he also wanted her to go on with her life, to be happy. Now standing in front of his stately marble tombstone, she felt reassured that it was okay for her to move forward.

Fog rolled in over the mountain from the coastal town of Pacifica, sending a chilly shudder up Sadie's neck. Coco hunkered down in her tote, giving Sadie an upward glance from the bag's opening. After a silent conversation with Morris, Sadie returned to her car and dropped back down to Hwy 101.

Sadie felt an energy that grew even stronger the closer she came to the airport. The sight of arriving and departing planes within the runway lights struck her as an endless choreographed dance of massive shiny jumbo jets.

She maneuvered her way into short-term parking and pulled into a spot just as another driver departed. Normally, people would pull up alongside the baggage claim portion of the terminal to wait in their cars for arriving friends, family, or colleagues. But that felt too impersonal for this occasion. She was eager to see Broussard and wanted to greet him in the airport.

With Coco safely settled inside her tote bag, Sadie headed for the terminal. Surrounded by the frenetic bustle of SFO, Sadie observed taxis lined up in designated zones at the curb while ride-share drivers occupied lesser desired spots back in the parking structure. Rolling suitcase wheels clacked against the sidewalk as arriving and departing passengers shouted greetings and goodbyes to family and friends. The flurry of activity fueled Sadie's already heightened sense of anticipation.

The arrival screen showed Broussard's plane to be about ten minutes out, just enough time for a quick cup of something chocolaty at a coffee stand she'd spotted on the way in. Knowing caffeine this late in the evening would keep her awake half the night, Sadie ordered a decaf mocha and grabbed two seats in the closest row of chairs, one for herself and one for Coco in the tote. She pulled a treat from a side pocket and dropped it inside, after which she linked her arm through the handles and cupped both hands around the cardboard cup. Sipping carefully after blowing across the beverage to cool it, an irritated, slightly familiar voice nearby caught her attention.

"Yes, of course I want to continue."

Sadie glanced over her shoulder at the row of seats that backed up against hers. A man with graying hair held a cell phone to his ear. He was bent forward, one arm propped on the back of his chair, and his face was hidden. Still, he looked and sounded a lot like Seymour Wainwright.

"Yes, I already told you. Don't worry. I've taken care of everything. Just as I said I would. We can meet up when I'm done handling a personal affair." He paused and listened. "None of your business," he snapped.

Taken care of what? Sadie wondered. *Roberta?* Hoping the conversation would continue with some clarifying statements, she soon knew she was out of luck. The man put his phone in a jacket pocket, stood, and walked in the direction of the rental car companies. Sadie rose and started to follow him. He spun around, returned to the row of seats, and picked up a paper bag he had forgotten before. She had a chance to study his face and realized he wasn't much taller than Sadie. Not Seymour Wainwright. She let the stranger go and stood in front of the flight information display, which showed Broussard's flight had arrived.

Sadie reached the baggage claim area as most passengers had already entered the terminal. Groups of travelers waited as suitcases descended the sloped conveyor belt. Sadie found herself wondering which bags Broussard's might be. Surely not the hot pink striped specimen tilting sideways. Or the camouflage duffel bag. Or a trio of matching suitcases in ascending order of size with teddy bear luggage tags.

It only took a moment to spot the tall, handsome detective standing to the side of the crowd. She smiled as he noticed her and approached.

"Ms. Kramer."

"Detective Broussard."

They both laughed, then exchanged an awkward hug.

"I'm delighted to be reminded of the face behind all those texts and phone calls," Broussard said.

"As am I," Sadie agreed. "And I apologize if I kept you waiting. I stopped for a decaf mocha and thought I saw someone. Seymour Wainwright, as a matter of fact."

"Really? So that *was* you in that tilted eavesdropping pose in the chairs near the coffee bar. I was about to come over and check."

"Guilty as charged," Sadie said. "I didn't think I was being that obvious."

"You forget what my job is." Broussard laughed and then became serious. "But you're not sure it was him? This would be the victim's husband, right?"

Sadie nodded. "Yes, Roberta's husband. But no, it wasn't him. I guess I'm a little too invested in the future of the Wainwright family, so I'm seeing ghosts everywhere." *Or goblins?* she thought. "Did you check any bags?"

"Just one that I already picked up, plus my carry-on." Broussard held a small hard-shell suitcase in one hand and grabbed the pull handle of another. "Always easiest to travel light for a short trip."

"Well, then right this way. I'm just back a few rows in short-term parking."

Once they reached the car, Sadie unlocked the doors and slid into the driver's seat. She popped the trunk so Broussard could put his luggage inside. After he shuffled the bags into place, he closed the trunk and slipped into the passenger seat, and they headed back north on Hwy 101.

Sadie tried to gather her thoughts about the Wainwright situation in order to discuss it now that Broussard was there. But she hesitated. It would be much easier to go over details after they got settled somewhere to talk, likely the next day, considering the late hour. Instead, she fell into small talk and pointed out an empty lot to the right of the freeway.

"That's where Candlestick Park once stood, home to the San Francisco 49ers and the S.F. Giants."

"Ah," Broussard said. "Aren't you full of surprises. You're a sports fan." Even in the dark, Sadie could tell he was smiling. She could hear it in his voice.

Sadie laughed. "I don't know if I'd go that far. My late husband was more of a sports fan. But I have fond memories of watching Willie "The Say Hey Kid" Mays play baseball there. Plenty of other big names played there too."

"Like Joe Montana," Broussard said. "And John Brodie. Great quarterbacks."

"Ah," Sadie said, imitating Broussard's prior response. "Football is your game, Detective Broussard." *Wow. My nerves must really be acting up to be talking sports.*

"Not that much. I watched a lot of New Orleans Saints games when I worked as a security support officer early in my career. It was always nice to be paid a full shift and get to watch a game at the same time."

They fell into a period of silence. *Fatigue? Nerves?* Sadie wasn't sure.

"Where are you staying?" Sadie asked, wondering what exit she needed to take in order to drop him off.

"The Grand Hyatt," Broussard said.

"Excellent choice," Sadie said. "Convenient to Union Square."

"Frogert suggested it, said it wasn't far from the Wainwright mansion," Broussard offered.

"That was nice of him."

"He also said it wasn't far from where you caused him trouble last time."

Sadie heard him chuckle faintly. "Not quite as nice of him," she mused. "We're not far. I can have you there in a few minutes. You must be tired after the long day and flight."

"I am, but actually, a thought occurred to me at the airport while we were preparing to land. I'm wondering if... this will sound crazy, considering how late it is..."

"Crazy is my middle name," Sadie said. She wasn't sure if she should be tickled or offended when he didn't counter the statement. But it was hardly a point of contention. She doubted many people thought her sane, herself included.

"Is there a chance you might want to drive past the mansion?"

Sadie didn't even hesitate. "Absolutely."

With that, all thought of small talk disappeared. She took the appropriate exit, and the two of them headed to the scene of the crime.

SIXTEEN

It was almost midnight when Sadie and Broussard pulled up in front of the mansion. Dark and shrouded in the fog that had rolled in earlier with the brisk ocean winds, the stately building looked like something out of a horror film, backlit by milky moonlight. Sadie hoped Broussard wasn't about to suggest they get out of the car and walk around.

At least the police tape had been removed, which took away a touch of what would have been an even creepier tableau. It also meant Froggy had cleared the scene, and she, Charlotte, and the rest of the crew would be able to start decorating inside the next day. That was a relief. Charlotte was determined that the Spooktacular would go on as planned in spite of her mother's death. They had an extraordinary amount of work to do in a tight time frame.

"It's a little creepy," Broussard said, almost as if he'd read her mind.

"Is that an official police assessment?" Sadie quipped.

"For this time of night, I'd say yes," Broussard replied. "Though I might alter it if I wrote an official report."

Sadie tilted her head sideways, an undetected gesture in the dark vehicle. "What would you write?"

"Quiet location on a large block of land. Lack of detailed view due to weather elements. No sign of anyone present. Wait." Broussard pointed to a clump of bushes. "Did you see that?"

"What?" Sadie's eyes followed the direction of his arm but didn't see anything out of the ordinary. Admittedly, she couldn't see much at all through the thick fog.

"There was movement in that cluster of shrubbery." Instinctively he slipped his right hand inside his jacket, and Sadie realized he could be armed. This made her feel both nervous and protected at the same time.

"Maybe it's just the wind," Sadie said. Half of her wanted this to be true simply for the sake of safety. The eeriness of the scene was already unnerving, and she was glad she wasn't alone. Yet the other half of her was attracted to the idea they might catch the murderer.

"I don't think so," Broussard said. "There's not even a light breeze, and those bushes were shaking steadily." Sadie could hear the concern in his voice.

A moment later, Sadie saw the movement herself, and she knew Broussard was right. Had it been gusty, the motion of bushes rustling might have made sense, but the air was still. And when a figure stepped out from behind the foliage and made its way quickly across the grounds, it was clear they weren't imagining it. Someone was sneaking around on the property.

"Stay here. Lock the doors." Broussard's tone told Sadie not to argue as he stepped out of the car. She pressed the door lock and, mimicking similar scenes from movies, slid down lower in her seat, keeping her eyes just high enough to watch him cross the lawn. Veering away from the cluster of bushes, he slipped off in the direction the figure had gone.

Sadie waited nervously, running possibilities through her mind. Who would have reason to be sneaking around at the mansion? And were they only on the property itself, or had they made their way inside? Was someone staking out the mansion and grounds looking for clues? Or were they there to conceal one left behind?

She ran her fingers along the controls on the side door and lowered the window a half inch or so and listened. A faint scuffle of shoes against dirt carried from the orchard, and sharp but muddled voices accompanied the sound of bushes rustling and branches breaking.

Although it felt like thirty minutes went by before Broussard returned, Sadie knew realistically it was no more than ten. A knock on the passenger window sent her heart pounding even though she'd anticipated the detective's return.

"Open the trunk," Broussard said through the window opening. He pointed toward the rear of the car. She pulled the latch and heard Broussard drop something heavy into the trunk. He slammed it shut and got back in the car.

"Not a body, I hope," Sadie said. "One is enough for this week."

"No," Broussard said. "Just a clunky object I hit my head on. It didn't seem to belong in the orchard. Some kind of camera or something on a tripod."

Sadie turned the interior light on, but Broussard immediately told her to shut it off. She did as he requested, but the brief illumination was enough to glimpse a gash on his forehead, a trickle of blood running down from it.

"What happened?" Shaken, the question was the best Sadie could manage. She rummaged through the car's side pockets and pulled out a travel pack of tissues. Plucking several from the small package, she reached out to press them against the wound. Broussard leaned away from her attempt at nursing but took the tissues from her.

"Not what I wanted to happen," Broussard said. "Whoever it was must have heard me coming and took cover. When

I spotted him lurking behind a tree, I called, 'Hey!' and he started running. So I tackled him into some bushes, and that's where I hit my head. I was stunned enough for him to get away."

"You said 'he,'" Sadie pointed out. "So it was a man?" She watched as Broussard shrugged his shoulders in the moonlit car.

"That's my guess," Broussard said, pressing the tissues against his forehead. "Tall, thin, and strong. Though I can't be sure."

"But I heard voices." Sadie considered this, wondering if she'd heard two distinct voices in spite of the sound not being clear.

"Just mine," Broussard said. "The trespasser only grunted a few times while we struggled. A smart move there, avoiding the chance of me hearing his voice."

"So it could have been anyone, even a vagrant. We do have a lot of homeless people here in the city."

"It doesn't matter now," Broussard said as he dropped his head back against the headrest. "I think it's time to drop me off at the hotel. Whoever it was is long gone."

* * *

Sadie dropped Broussard off. Had it been earlier, they would likely have taken advantage of the hotel's upscale setting to enjoy a late-night drink. But considering late night was now early morning, they said a quick goodbye, and Sadie drove home.

"Sorry, Coco, quite a long day for you," Sadie said as she fluffed up the plush dog bed and set her down. Coco looked up and eyed Sadie sleepily. "For me too, you know. For a lot of us, especially Broussard."

As Sadie changed into her pink flamingo pajamas, she tried to comprehend the totality of her favorite detective's day, starting with work in New Orleans, then the plane flight to San Francisco, the visit to the mansion and subsequent skirmish with the trespasser, to finally being dropped off at the hotel, gashed forehead and all. Now *that* was a long day. It would have been even longer if he'd accepted Sadie's suggestion to take him to the emergency room to make sure the head injury didn't require stitches. She didn't blame him for objecting. Once they were in decent light, the wound looked more dramatic than deep, and he was certainly in need of a good night's rest, whatever was left of it.

Snuggling under the soft duvet on her bed, she expected to fall asleep immediately out of sheer exhaustion. Instead, her brain perked up in that annoying way that only gets worse once the wish for sleep becomes more intense. She rolled from side to side, hoping a different position would help but to no avail. Finally she padded to the kitchen, fixed a cup of herbal tea, and settled down with it in the living room. From her wing-backed chair, she could look out over the now opaque city landscape and think.

Tall and strong. That was the only description Broussard was able to give of his assailant. Sadie took a sip of tea and thought this over. Cooper was tall and physically fit; he'd certainly have the physical ability to tackle and run.

Seymour was tall—like son, like father—though his age made it less likely he would be able to escape what Sadie was now thinking of as Broussard's Tackle. Or did it? Sadie quickly reprimanded herself for this thought. Since both she and Broussard were in the same general demographic as Seymour, she shouldn't discount his abilities so readily. But why would he be sneaking around on his own property? For that matter, why would Cooper?

Guy Bijou was also tall, but while he was wiry and maybe strong, he didn't seem like the type of person who would get into any kind of physical altercation. He was simply too... She didn't know quite how to describe it. Meek, maybe?

It might have made sense for Dwight, the caretaker, to be on the property, even at that late hour if some kind of immediate repair was needed. But he would have had a work light, and he'd have no reason to run. Besides, he was stout of build, not thin.

Then again, Broussard hadn't been sure the trespasser was male. Charlotte was tall and lanky, and she hardly struck Sadie as a weakling. In the dark, without hearing her voice, Broussard could have mistaken her for a man if she thrashed around enough for him to be unable to get a good hold on her. Maggie, on the other hand, was far too short to match the description.

Anxious to discuss these possibilities with Broussard the next day, Sadie finished her tea and returned to bed, finally falling asleep.

SEVENTEEN

An early morning buzzing woke Sadie from an odd dream. All the potential suspects in Roberta Wainwright's murder had been lined up behind the bush she and Broussard had observed moving the night before, but the bush had stretched into a longer hedge. Bright light illuminated their faces in such a way as to resemble a police lineup. Each face was well-defined, but the bodies were hidden behind the shrubbery. Odder still, they were all exactly the same height, as if blocks of wood had been propped below each person in an attempt to minimize the chance of identifying the guilty party. Sadie had been seated across from the lineup on an antique couch in keeping with the historic time period of the mansion. A kitchen timer tick-tocked as it dangled from a tree branch, counting down the time Sadie had to pick out the correct suspect.

Pushing the dream aside, Sadie sat up in bed and grabbed the phone on her nightstand, finding the waiting text.

Ms. Kramer

She yawned, stretched, and then sent a reply.

Detective Broussard

I'm meeting Frogert this morning for coffee to compare notes. I'll catch up with you later today.

How's the forehead? Sadie pondered the omission of an invite to have coffee with them, but police business was police business. If they were meeting at the precinct where they could talk privately, there would be no reason to include her. However, it was possible...

Sore but fine. The hotel desk gave me a Band-Aid to cover the gash. Unfortunately, it has bats on it. It's all they had.

Sadie resisted the urge to burst out laughing, then reminded herself this was a text and he couldn't hear. The resulting guffaw was enough to send Coco springing from her dog bed.

From the children's first aid box, I take it.

I suppose so.

I'm sure it's a good look for you. Sadie snickered again.

Possibly. But I plan to switch it out for a normal bandage as soon as I track one down.

Where's the fun in that? Sadie made a mental note to track down some bat bandages for herself. How had she managed to not be aware something that cool existed?

Gotta go. Will text later.

Okay. Sadie sent the text off and pondered the meeting. Certainly she knew better than to try to crash a meeting at the precinct. That was private. But if they just happened to be meeting at the Java Sun Café... well, that was a different situation.

"Up and at 'em, Coco," Sadie said, heading for the kitchen. Coco trotted along right behind her, eager for her breakfast, which Sadie promptly served. While the pup downed her morning meal, Sadie clicked the coffee maker on and then rummaged through her closet for something to wear.

"Hmm," she said to no one in particular. "Not too fancy, not too plain." Hangers clattered against each other until she pulled out a blue denim skirt with rhinestone-trimmed pockets and an off-white jersey top with raglan sleeves. She had the perfect flats to match the outfit, which she fetched from her sizable shoe collection. With a mischievous smile, she searched through her drawer of casual jewelry and found a small black brooch in the shape of a bat, which she clipped near the neckline.

Back in the kitchen, Sadie poured a half cup of the freshly brewed coffee and clicked the coffee maker off as she sipped it. The meager amount of the brewed beverage would be enough to get her to her destination, where, of course, there would be plenty more.

"Let's go, Coco." Upon hearing the word *go*, and seeing a leash come off a wall hook, the Yorkie yipped with delight and ran two full circles around Sadie before attempting to hop into the open tote bag on her own. The admirable but unsuccessful move sent Coco back on the ground, where she stomped a tiny paw and looked at Sadie dejectedly.

Scooping Coco up off the floor, Sadie got her settled in the tote. She checked her hair and makeup in a mirror, gathered her keys, and headed out.

The Java Sun Café was busy when she arrived. All tables were occupied, and additional customers leaned against a long counter by the front window. It only took a moment to spot the two detectives, who were hunched over cups of coffee, deep in conversation. So intent were they on their discussion that they didn't see Sadie until she stood at their table.

"All the tables are taken, it seems," she said, glancing around innocently. "But I do see an extra chair here." She accented the statement with a sweet smile.

Broussard and Frogert exchanged glances. Broussard raised his hands, palms out, in a gesture that claimed innocence.

"It's true," Sadie said. "He had no idea I'd be here. I didn't even know myself."

Frogert simply sighed and pulled out the empty chair. After excusing herself for a quick trip to the counter to place an order for a latte, Sadie returned and took the seat, doing her best to keep quiet while their conversation continued.

Sadie tried to understand the back-and-forth between the two detectives, but she suspected they were purposefully using jargon that might confuse her. From what she gathered, while Guy Bijou had been under investigation for untoward shenanigans on the set of his show, he was cleared of criminal wrongdoing. Broussard believed Bijou was innocent in the New Orleans case, but some things didn't quite add up, and trouble, of the paranormal variety, seemed to follow Guy wherever he went. Broussard wondered if someone was trying to sabotage Guy's show. A rival, maybe? He wasn't sure. But he knew he didn't want anyone else to be hurt.

If I were a less subtle person, I'd be taking notes. Sadie was surprised the two detectives hadn't chased her away yet. Broussard seemed to have a great respect for Detective Frogert, which made Sadie look at him in a different light. Despite the bad mustache, the rumpled suit, the terrible habits he had of tapping pens and shrinking away from tiny dogs, maybe Froggy was a good egg after all. She wondered if he had a first name. She should know, surely. It would be on his business card.

They had somehow veered off the topic of Guy Bijou and his *Ghosts and Goblins* show and were now discussing the differences in procedure between the New Orleans police department and the San Francisco police department.

Sadie began to tune out and found herself watching other customers in the café. She smiled as a young, obviously pregnant mother drew in a small sketchpad with her daughter, who must have been about three. The mother wore a pair of maternity overalls, and one strap had slid off her shoulder and down her arm. The little girl's dark ringlets fell into her face as she leaned over the sketchpad and pressed a colored pencil to the paper. The mother tucked a strand of the girl's hair behind her ear.

Off to the right in a corner on the opposite side of the café, a couple sat, hands clasped across the table, talking intently and staring into each other's eyes. *What a lovely sight!* Sadie thought. They were middle-aged, the woman in her forties, the man his fifties or sixties. The man raised the woman's hands and pressed his lips against her knuckles. She yanked her hands away and leaned back in her chair, her black hair swinging as if it were angry. *Maybe not so lovely. She looks a little bit like Maggie Barton.* She watched the couple a little longer and stared a little harder as she sipped her latte. Was her mind playing tricks on her? The man strongly resembled Seymour Wainwright. She seemed to be imagining him everywhere she went.

"Where are you, Ms. Kramer?" Broussard asked, his tone playful. He reached out and rubbed her hand.

Sadie swallowed hard, and her drink nearly went down the wrong way. "Drowning in my inane thoughts, Detective Broussard." She glanced at Froggy. "I see you rolling your eyes, Detective."

"Who could blame me in the face of such flirting?"

Broussard laughed and nodded at Frogert. "Let's get going, shall we? We should find Bijou before he causes any more damage even if he doesn't understand what he's doing."

Both men stood, both left cash tips on the table. Sadie stood too.

Broussard put his hand on her shoulder. "No. You need to stay here. Or go to your boutique, or home, or to the chocolate place you're always talking about. I'll call you when we know more."

"But—" Sadie sputtered.

"No," Broussard said. "You're smart, and you can be helpful. But I want you to be safe. I'll see you later." He looked into the tote bag on the extra chair at their table. "Coco," he said. "Tell Sadie to stay."

The two detectives doffed invisible hats to Sadie and left the café. She sat back down and took a deep, deep breath.

"Well, Coco, what do you make of that? Sidelined not by one but by two perfectly adequate detectives." She gazed back toward the couple she'd been watching, but the man was gone and the woman was gathering up her things. Sadie was hoping she could get a good look at her. She'd only seen Maggie once in person. The photograph on her desk didn't really count. When she saw her at the Wainwright gardens, she'd been moving pretty quickly. She watched closely until the woman turned so that Sadie could see her face. It was, indeed, Maggie Barton.

She took another sip of her latte. It was cold. "Coco," she whispered, "we've been uninvited to the boys' club." She stopped herself and drank some water. "Okay. That's not fair. There is no boys' club. It's just a detectives' club. I guess they're afraid I'll mess up their investigation. But I think it's time for you and me to do our own investigating. Let's see if we can track Ms. Barton down at the foundation headquarters." Coco barked from her hidden spot in the middle of the tote bag, but a dish crashing to the floor covered the noise. "Right you are, Coco. Let's quit this joint before we spy any more people we know canoodling."

EIGHTEEN

S adie and Coco entered the lobby of the Wainwright headquarters and made their way up to the second floor, where they heard the sound of a woman's voice. "That must be Maggie, Coco," she said to the opening of her bag. "Let's just tiptoe into her office to see what's going on with her." She found Maggie on the phone, but when she saw Sadie, she gestured for her to join her. As she spoke, she fidgeted with a glittery sequined mask that lay on her desk.

"I so appreciate that," she said into the mouthpiece. "Yes, it's been really hard. I'm barely keeping it together. Thank you. And I'll see you at the party." After she hung up, she stood and shook Sadie's hand. "I'm happy to see you again, Ms. Kramer. I'm sorry we didn't get to speak before."

"Please, call me Sadie."

"All right, Sadie. Is there something I can do for you?"

"No, I was about to ask you the same thing."

"I'm fine, really," Maggie said. "It's all so awful though, you know? Roberta didn't deserve to die like that, to be *murdered*. She wasn't the kind of person anyone would want dead." Sadie wondered if this was true. Maggie inhaled deeply and let the breath out slowly as if she were practicing a form of meditation.

"I agree that it's horrifying." Sadie wondered if Maggie knew she had been the one to find Roberta. "I know you're probably really busy with all the planning for the Spooktacular and managing other foundation business, but I wanted to ask you about something." Sadie wasn't sure how to broach the subject of what she'd witnessed at the café. She decided to be direct. "I just came from the Java Sun Café, where I had a meeting with Detective Frogert and a friend."

"Oh." Maggie sat back down and folded her arms on her desk. "Then you saw me with Seymour Wainwright. And you say that detective was there? Did *he* notice us?"

Sadie shook her head. "I wasn't sure it was you *or* Seymour at first. But now I see you're wearing the same delightful skirt and that beautiful silver crab brooch I saw on the woman at the corner table."

Sadie was itching to hear Maggie's story. She realized her "investigating" was a terrible habit and possibly annoying to others, but it made her feel more alive, more helpful. She wondered if she should have taken the same career path as Keith Cross, the journalistic path. "That detective came calling here again the other day. We had quite a bruising conversation."

"I'm sorry to hear that," Sadie said. "Detective Frogert can be quite dogged when he's investigating a murder." Coco whined from inside her carrier when she heard the word *dogged*. Maggie looked a little surprised but said nothing about the out-of-place sound.

"You've dealt with him before?" she asked.

"I have."

"Did he treat you like a suspect?"

"Detective Frogert treats everyone like a suspect, even baristas, even preschoolers drawing in their sketchpads."

"I suppose that's sort of comforting."

"Is there anything I can help you sort through? Did Detective Frogert have a specific reason for questioning you again?" Sadie asked. She knew, of course, why Froggy had interviewed Maggie a second time, but Maggie had no way of knowing what Sadie knew. Did she?

Maggie sighed. "Well, you see, someone stole something from my desk, something private." She paused and scratched at an imaginary bug bite on her left wrist. "It was a letter, a note, really, and it might be kind of incriminating."

Might be? Sadie thought.

"The person who took it passed it on to that detective, and now he thinks I have a reason for wanting Roberta dead."

Don't you?

"My dear girl!" Sadie tried to find a decent way to phrase her next question. "The note was from Seymour?"

Maggie looked a bit faint. "How did you know?"

"I'm just piecing things together as I go. Will it help you to talk through it?"

"This has been such a strange and trying day. Well, week." She picked the mask up again and played with the elastic band. "I suppose it couldn't hurt to get some of this out."

"So," Sadie began, "were you and Seymour in love?"

"I'll tell you what I told that detective, though I don't think he believed me. Seymour was very kind to me during a difficult time in my life." Maggie's voice shook a bit. "My father had just passed away, and I wasn't handling it well." She picked up the photo Sadie had noticed the other day, then put it back down. "Seymour started doing me small favors. For instance, he once took time out of his busy day to give me a ride to pick up my car when it was in the shop. And he bought me a beautiful suit for my birthday. From your boutique, I believe. He and Roberta could often be generous in that way with people in their circle. I didn't realize Seymour's feelings toward me were romantic, I guess because I was in mourning and simply wasn't paying attention. When he expressed his affection, I told him we couldn't be in a relationship, partly because of Roberta and partly because I just wasn't interested."

Sadie nodded. "When did you receive Seymour's note?"

"I found it on my desk the day after Roberta died. He must have left it there before his trip to Houston. I hadn't been in the office for a couple of days."

"Can I ask why you met with Seymour at the café?"

"Oh, Sadie, he was in anguish." Maggie, too, looked as if she were in anguish. "He called me as soon as he got back into town. He told me he couldn't believe that Roberta had died, and he couldn't understand how anyone could *kill* her. But then he made it clear that his feelings for me hadn't waned. He felt such guilt. So I agreed to meet with him to put this monstrous situation to bed once and for all."

Sadie cringed internally at Maggie's choice of a cliché. "And did you?"

"Yes, for now. He said even if I did return his feelings, this would not be the time for us to begin a romance, that we would have to wait through a mourning period."

"But did he understand that you're not interested?"

"I think so. I'm hoping that time will erase some of his feelings of remorse and his affection for me. I told him I'm in love with someone else." She traced the eye sockets of the mask. "This is such a strange time. Roberta murdered, Seymour in agony *and* feeling guilty basically for being human, the Spooktacular going on despite what happened."

She lifted the mask and gazed at it as if she were studying someone's face. Sadie felt a shudder creep up from deep inside her stomach. The mask looked just like the one that had covered Roberta's face.

"Maggie?" Maggie put the mask down and looked at Sadie,

waiting for her next question. "Where did you get that mask?"

"Isn't it pretty? Seymour gave it to me last week. He told me I might think about wearing it to the Spooktacular."

"I see," Sadie said.

They stopped talking and sat quietly for a bit.

"I know who found the note and who turned it over to the police," Maggie finally said.

"Do you?" Sadie lifted her tote bag into her lap and reached in to pet Coco.

"It was Charlotte Wainwright. She started snooping around my office as soon as Roberta asked her to help with the Spooktacular. I don't know what she expected to find. I've always consider her a friend. I think she thought Roberta was going to replace her with me in their will." Maggie's laugh was brittle. "I overheard them last week, shouting at each other."

Sadie did wonder at all the arguing Charlotte seemed to do. "Roberta and Charlotte?"

"Yes. I was just arriving at work, and I heard voices coming from my office of all places. I didn't want to disturb a private discussion between mother and daughter, so I waited in the hall."

She paused again, rose, and went to a small refrigerator in the corner of the office where she pulled out two bottles of water. She offered one to Sadie. "To me, it sounded like they *hated* each other."

"What do you mean?" Sadie asked.

"Roberta yelled that Charlotte was a slouching giraffe of a girl, and Charlotte screamed back that Roberta had no right to reduce her inheritance. Roberta said Charlotte hadn't *earned* it since she hadn't been as involved in the foundation and other family activities as her brother. She said at least Cooper had *tried*."

Sadie swallowed hard. "Did you really hear Roberta say she was going to reduce Charlotte's inheritance? Could she even do that without Seymour's blessing?"

"I'm not sure. I know Roberta had her own trust. She often joked about writing everyone out of it in order to leave the entire inheritance from her father to the foundation. But I don't know anything about wills or trusts or whatever. I just know that the fury in my office was palpable after they left."

"Did they see you?"

"Yes, of course. Charlotte stormed out and ran past me. When I got into my office, Roberta was sitting at my desk, gazing out the window." Maggie sighed again. "She said, 'I wish Charlotte were more like you, Maggie. You're elegant and calm. You wear your clothes well, and you're so efficient.' I didn't know what to say, but my instinct was to defend Charlotte. So I told her I think Charlotte is beautiful and that I admire Charlotte for the kind of work she does."

"How did she respond?" Sadie could hardly believe she was getting so much of Maggie's story. And Charlotte's!

"She laughed at me. 'That's another thing I like about you, Maggie. You're oh so diplomatic.'" Maggie glanced at a small gold-colored clock on her desk. "You know what, Sadie? I think I feel a bit better. I'm happy you stopped by."

"I'm glad." Sadie, too, felt a bit better.

Maggie's phone rang. "I'm so sorry," she said. "I'm afraid I have to take this."

"It's fine, it's fine!" Sadie let herself out of the building. She suspected Charlotte was already at the mansion trying not to panic, so she needed to be on her way.

NINETEEN

Sadie spotted Charlotte as soon as she pulled up in front of the Wainwright mansion. Looking more frantic than the last time she'd seen her, the young woman stood on the marble steps to the mansion, one arm waving in the direction of the orchard in a swishing motion, the other pressing a cell phone against her ear. Cooper appeared from inside, set a cardboard carton on the porch, plucked his own phone out of his pocket, and disappeared back inside. Charlotte sent an annoyed look over her shoulder and pushed the box toward the edge of the top step. She finished whatever nonverbal commands she was giving workers—Sadie assumed the swishing arm was aimed at humans, not trees—and then propped her free arm on her hip. Noticing Sadie had pulled up, she began motioning again, this time with a gesture that said "hurry up." Sadie locked the car and walked up to meet her.

"I can't believe we only have one full day to finish everything," Charlotte sputtered as she slid her phone into a pocket of her linen pants. "I don't know how Mother handled these big events without going crazy. And that was without the police, the press, and hundreds of condolence phone calls to deal with. Thank heavens Maggie is handling most of those." Sadie noticed Charlotte's voice tightened at the mention of Maggie's name. She wondered if Charlotte had talked to Maggie, or her father, about the letter.

"Just tell me how I can help," Sadie said.

Charlotte looked around, appearing to debate options before finally pointing to the carton on the top step. "I need to meet with the caterer in the kitchen. Rescue her is more like it. Could you take this box around to the back garden? Dwight should be there waiting for it."

"Not a problem," Sadie said. She propped the tote bag on top of the box and stooped down to lift it, pleased to find it wasn't terribly heavy, although not entirely light. She'd be able to handle it. When she stood back up, Charlotte had already disappeared inside. "Okay, Coco. Looks like you're going for a ride." As usual upon hearing her name, Coco's head popped up out of the tote and remained there as they made their way around the side of the mansion. Coco yipped several greetings at two workmen who were installing light fixtures below trees in the orchard. She showed equal enthusiasm as Sadie approached the caretaker.

"Aha," Dwight said. "Those must be the pumpkins."

A little lightweight for pumpkins, Sadie thought. "I honestly have no idea," she said. "Charlotte asked me to bring the box back here."

Dwight laughed. "Let me guess. She sounded panicked."

"I'd say that's accurate," Sadie said. "Possibly even an understatement."

Dwight took the box and held it while Sadie lifted the still-yipping tote bag off the top. He set the carton on the ground, pulled a Swiss Army knife out of his pocket, and sliced through the packaging tape. Replacing the knife in his pocket, he opened the top flaps. "Yep, just as I thought. Same ones we've used before."

Sadie peered into the box, noting clear plastic bags with scrunched-up orange paper inside. She ran possibilities through her mind. "Some kind of lantern?"

Dwight nodded. "Exactly. Paper lanterns. These will hang throughout the garden. We do this every year. They're quite impressive at night, especially with twinkling lights below them."

"Is that what they're setting up in the orchard? The workmen over there looked pretty focused when I passed by."

"Nope," Dwight said. "That's an entirely different plan. Those guys are arranging spotlights at the base of some of the trees to showcase flying monkeys up above."

"Flying monkeys?" Sadie ran the image through her mind. "Not your everyday Halloween decoration, that's for sure. You mean like the ones in *The Wizard of Oz*?"

"Yes," Dwight said. "Except these aren't *like* the ones in the movie. These *are* the ones in the movie. Some of them anyway. Maggie's grandfather worked lighting for MGM, and he was able to keep some of the props from that scene. Had them hanging in his garage. Scared her half to death as a child."

"How fascinating," Sadie said. "Isn't she worried they might get stolen? Entertainment memorabilia can be valuable."

Dwight shook his head. "They'll be high up in the trees. The spotlights will beam up at them, but no one will be able to reach them. Plus there are only a few. We even have a security guard assigned to each one." He propped a ladder next to a lamppost and climbed up several steps. Sadie noticed a string of tiny lights wrapped around the post. "Could you hand me one of those lanterns from the box? Just tear off the plastic wrapping and stretch the paper out."

"Got it." Sadie opened one of the packages and stretched the orange accordion-style paper folds until they formed a pumpkin shape. "Wow, these are huge." She reached up, and Dwight took the lantern from her hand.

"They need to be," Dwight said. Fluffing the shape a bit more, he took out his knife again and cut a slit partway up the back, just enough to allow the paper form to slip over the lamppost's light.

"Clever," Sadie said, envisioning what the garden would look like in the dark once all the lampposts turned into glowing pumpkins. The twinkling lights below each one would render the setting almost magical. It was a perfect outdoor plan: an enchanted garden and a spooky orchard. Something for everyone even without stepping inside the mansion itself.

The sound of Cooper's voice interrupted Sadie's thoughts, and she turned to see him sticking his phone back in his pocket. He was dressed in casual business attire and sported a smirk that Sadie wasn't terribly fond of.

"I'll take over from here," Cooper said. "Dwight and I are used to setting these up together." Sadie was relieved that Cooper had come around to the idea of the Spooktacular going on despite his mother's death. At least there would be no more fights over that. "We need time for a little man-to-man chat anyway. And you're needed in the kitchen."

Sadie bristled. "Hopefully you're not saying that's where a woman's place is." Coco, hearing the tone of Sadie's voice, let out a yip of backup support.

"Certainly not," Cooper said. "I know better than to even hint at something like that. But it may be a woman's place to stop my sister from throwing dishes at the wall or strangling Elaine, the head caterer. Charlotte is on quite the warpath. Something about a missing punch bowl. My efforts to calm her down failed miserably. Maybe you'll have better luck."

"On my way," Sadie said, not surprised to hear Charlotte was on a rampage. The woman had seemed on the edge of coming unglued the last time she'd talked to her. Granted, losing her mother had to be distressing. But it felt like more was going on behind Charlotte's outbursts. She thought back to the screaming argument Maggie had shared with Sadie. Just how angry with Roberta had her daughter been?

Sadie hoisted her tote bag's handle over her shoulder and headed around to the front of the mansion. Climbing the marble stairs at a quick pace, she entered the building. Even if she hadn't found the kitchen when she searched the mansion the day Roberta died, it would have been easy to find. She simply followed Charlotte's screaming voice.

"If it's not here now, how do I know it'll be here in time for the Spooktacular?"

Sadie entered cautiously, prepared to duck if anything happened to go airborne. She found Charlotte pacing, both hands raking through her hair. A young woman in her late twenties stood with her back pressed against a long counter. She was of medium height, a slender but shapely build, and more than slightly attractive. She appeared calm on the surface but gripped a clipboard more securely than necessary.

"Everything will be here for the event, Ms. Wainwright. This is just the first of several deliveries."

"Well, I certainly hope so, Elaine! That's what we're paying you for!" Charlotte released two fists of hair from her grip and let her arms drop by her side. She rolled her eyes as she passed Sadie and whispered, "She's all yours."

Sadie watched the young caterer visibly relax at Charlotte's exit. The woman waved her clipboard at Sadie but said nothing.

"How can I help?"

"You can convince that woman that everything ordered will be here on time. It's scheduled in several deliveries, not everything at once. I know the family has had a terrible shock, but Roberta had everything planned perfectly. It's all detailed in the event itinerary." Again she waved the clipboard. "Her daughter doesn't need to freak out like she is."

More footsteps. Another voice.

"Everything okay in here?" Maggie said as she entered.

"Not really," Elaine said. "Charlotte is being unreasonable."

"Try not to blame her for being stressed," Maggie said. "This week hasn't exactly gone according to plan."

Not true, Sadie mused. *It has gone according to someone's plan. But whose?*

"It's not easy to work under these conditions," Elaine said. "I'm just trying to do my job. Charlotte continues to go berserk and scream, Mr. Wainwright—the older one, Roberta's husband—says he's too busy to deal with anything Roberta set up, and Cooper keeps hitting on me."

Maggie seemed momentarily taken aback but recovered quickly. "I'll talk to each of them. Sadie can assist with whatever you need right now." Not waiting for confirmation from Sadie, Maggie mouthed the words "thank you" and left the room.

"So, Elaine, is it?" Sadie said, turning back to the caterer.

"Yes."

"What can I do to help?"

"Can you just make sure the items on the counter match the delivery list?" Elaine pointed to an array of chafing dishes, bowls, and serving utensils.

"No problem." Sadie took the clipboard, compared the list to the objects on the counter, and checked each one off. She returned the paperwork. "Anything else?"

"How about making this family a little less crazy?"

Sadie sighed as she watched the caterer walk away. *Probably not going to happen.*

TWENTY

Tensions continued to run high wherever Charlotte made an appearance, and Sadie, though she thought of herself as a generally patient person, needed a break before she ended up doing a little panicked screaming herself.

"Dwight?" she called to the caretaker, who was on a ladder in the courtyard, replacing a light bulb. "Coco and I are going out, just for a bit. We'll be back soon."

He waved at her. She lifted Coco out of her tote, clipped on the sparkly leash, and carried her tiny companion through the mansion and into the grayish afternoon.

"Let's go for a short walk, Coco. It's time to take a break from all the drama in there, don't you think?"

They strolled down the steps and wandered into the gardens. It felt good to be outside in the relative quiet. At least the noises she could hear—passing traffic mostly—were steady and almost soothing. She knew she couldn't stay away long or someone would come looking for her. Possibly to break up a fight? She chuckled at the thought.

What would Broussard think of all this chaos? She wished he were here with her, helping, or that she could be with him, investigating. Yes, that sounded more like it. They could go over all the information each of them had gathered in the past couple of days. She could tell him about Maggie; he could tell her what he and Froggy had discovered about Guy. That is, if he'd be willing to share.

"Do you think Maggie was telling the truth, Coco? She doesn't *seem* to be a liar. But when it comes to murder, even the nicest people could find it necessary to mislead others. Her situation with Seymour is awfully complicated. It's like a whole soap opera storyline all on its own."

She turned back toward the mansion and started up the stairs. Suddenly she remembered that feeling she'd had the afternoon she found Roberta and faced Froggy's scrutiny. She remembered the weakness from the shock of it all, and that shock hit her all over again. She sat on one of the steps, pulled Coco into her lap, and buried her face in her soft Yorkie fur. Coco licked her cheek several times. "Ah. That's better. Nothing a little dog's love can't cure."

When she looked up, she saw a tall, thin figure sprinting toward her from the direction of the orchard. "Oh dear, Coco. What now?"

Guy Bijou stopped in front of her in baggy jeans, his strange hat perched on his head. "Hello, Ms. Kramer. Might I speak with you?" He sat down next to her and patted Coco, who growled but then licked his hand.

Sadie wondered if the dog sensed paranormal activity following Guy around. *Nonsense. He probably just seems weird to her. After all, he is a bit odd.* "You might if you'll call me Sadie. I think you know by now I prefer it to Ms. Kramer."

"Of course!"

"What can I do for you, Guy?"

"I have a problem. This Dwight fellow keeps chasing me out of the mansion and off the grounds. He seems to think I'm trespassing, even though I've explained that I'm not. All I want to do is take a tour of the mansion to see if I can detect any unusual activity," Guy said. He plucked his hat off his head and crushed it between his long hands.

Sounds a lot like trespassing to me. "There's a lot of unusual activity going on in there, for sure," she said. "I don't think you want to risk being caught in the cross fire."

Guy laughed. "No, I mean *paranormal* activity, Sadie."

"I know what you mean. Don't you think it would be more appropriate for you to investigate your ghosts or goblins another time? Or maybe even probe another location?"

Guy reshaped his hat and plopped it back on his head. "I don't think you understand. I was asked to investigate the mansion for a story that might end up on *Guy's Ghosts and Goblins* once the producers agree to renew the series."

This surprised Sadie. "Really? Was it Roberta Wainwright who asked you."

"No!"

Was Guy frightened at the sound of Roberta's name? Sadie wondered. His reaction seemed strong, and he appeared edgy.

"It was her husband, Seymour. He contacted me months ago and talked about the Spooktacular, told me about the mansion's legends. He thought it would be good publicity if the mansion appeared on my show, either before or after the party. But then, er..." He seemed to be having trouble finding his words. "Well, we had an incident on one show in New Orleans, so it's been off the air for a while."

"I heard something about that from my friend, Detective Broussard."

Guy winced. "Yes, the detective and I are well acquainted."

"So I understand." Sadie resisted the urge to laugh. She suddenly had the sensation of being a school principal speaking with a student who'd been sent to her office. "Go on."

"I knew the date of the event, and I contacted Seymour and offered to come do some research, and he was all for it. But the caretaker keeps telling his staff to run me off. I haven't seen Seymour at all, and he hasn't been returning my calls, so he can't back me up. I'm not even sure what he looks like. I've only emailed with him and spoken to him on the phone."

"You could always Google him," Sadie suggested. "You'd come up with an image, I'm sure. But you'll know him by his tailored suit and general air of appearing to own the place. Which, of course, he does. And his cigar. He carries around a cigar."

"Do you think you could convince Dwight that I'm not the enemy? Could you vouch for me? It's really hard to investigate paranormal activity in a mansion when I'm not allowed *inside* the mansion," Guy said.

"I'll see what I can do."

"I also have a bit of a confession to make, and I think because you're not part of the Wainwright family or officially on the staff I can tell you."

Sadie raised her eyebrows, and Coco sneezed. "What have you done, Guy?"

"I'm afraid I might have scared someone last night. I came to the mansion when I was sure everyone would be gone, and I searched the grounds and tried to find a way into the building."

"You didn't! What time was this?"

"Around midnight."

Was Sadie going to have to turn Guy in for attempted breaking and entering? Was there even such a crime? Or would trespassing be enough? Broussard and Froggy were already suspicious of Guy. Broussard was more forgiving, but he might not be once he learned Guy was the body he'd tackled in the gardens where he acquired the gash on his forehead. A terrible thought occurred to Sadie. "Guy, do you know you assaulted a police officer last night?"

He turned himself fully toward her. "What? What are you talking about?"

"Did the person you think you scared chase you through the orchard? And did he then try to tackle you? And did you then shake him off so that he fell and injured his head? And did you then run away, effectively resisting arrest?"

Guy's mouth dropped open. "I… I had no idea that was a police officer. He didn't identify himself."

"He needed all his breath to chase you. And, by the way, that was Detective Broussard."

Guy slapped his hand against his forehead. "Oh, no, no, no! This is *terrible*. All I wanted to do was try to find out if the mansion was haunted, help Seymour with whatever publicity he needs, and hopefully get my show back on the air. It feels like trouble is following me around everywhere these past months."

"Maybe you're being haunted by spirits from your past shows," Sadie said. She stood and picked up Coco. "I've got to get back in there. You're welcome to come with me to see if they'll trust my judgment."

"Really?" A look of hope crossed Guy's face.

"Sure, why not?" Did *she* trust Guy? Mostly. She liked him, and trouble could be like a poltergeist, she supposed. "You can always help me deal with Charlotte Wainwright. She's not handling being in charge very well. In fact, I think she just might be possessed."

TWENTY-ONE

Sadie hooked her free hand around Guy's elbow, more as a way to protect him than her. She cradled Coco with her right arm. They made their way through to the kitchen, which was where the noise was loudest. "Brace yourself, Guy. I think you're about to meet the original goblin." Sadie wasn't trying to be mean about Charlotte. She understood what the poor girl was going through. But the only other time she'd witnessed such extravagant bullying was when she shadowed a friend of hers who worked as a sous-chef in a famous kitchen where the head chef was a tyrant.

As soon as they entered, everyone in the kitchen—Elaine the caterer, Cooper, Maggie, and two young men who were carrying boxes in from another entrance—twirled and looked anxiously in their direction.

Charlotte jabbed her finger at Guy, a repetition of the gesture she'd made when she first met him a couple of days before. "And just what are *you* doing here? Sadie? What is *he* doing here? What do you think you're doing inviting this intruder, this *charlatan*, into our *home*."

Sadie thought it wise not to point out that no one lived in the mansion, so she wasn't sure it could be considered a home. "Guy actually has a right and a reason to be here, Charlotte. He was asked."

"Who asked him? The caterer? Can he find the missing napkins?"

Elaine stepped forward. "Ms. Wainwright, I told you, the napkins will be here before six, same as the punch bowl."

"Right!" Charlotte seemed to be spinning from one person to the other. Sadie almost expected her head to burst into flames at any moment. What happened to the kindness she thought she'd glimpsed during their quiet conversation the other day?

Sadie patted Guy's hand. If she'd been him, she would have been trembling in the face of Charlotte's formidable, grief-induced rage, and not much frightened Sadie. Coco was certainly shivering. But he stood straighter than she'd yet seen him. "It was your father, Charlotte, your father invited Guy to the mansion," she said.

"What are you *talking* about? My father would do no such thing."

"He's quite the fan of my show," Guy said.

"Be quiet, you," Charlotte snapped.

"Mr. Wainwright asked me to investigate whether the mansion might be infested with some kind of spirit," Guy said. "He wants this place to be featured on *Guy's Ghosts and Goblins.*"

"I thought you were canceled," Cooper said.

"Let's call it *on hiatus*," Guy replied. He frowned.

A burly, flushed man came to the kitchen doorway. "Has anyone seen Dwight? I need to use his car to pick up the dry ice, but the spare key isn't in the front drawing room desk where he usually keeps it. Could use a little help." He looked from Charlotte to Cooper to Maggie. Cooper and Maggie both shrugged and exchanged a glance.

"Good grief, Tommy!" Charlotte said to the man. "All these tiny little errors and distractions are making me crazy! I want this party to be perfect in honor of Mother, but at this rate, we'll never be finished, and everything will be a disaster!" She stalked to a bulletin board next to the large refrigerator-freezer, plucked a set of keys off a hook, and tossed them to Tommy. He caught them deftly in one hand.

"Thanks Ms. Wainwright. Sorry for the trouble."

Charlotte stood staring after Tommy. She was quite still, her back to everyone in the room, until her shoulders began to shake, and a sob escaped her thin body. Sadie was hobbled from action because she still held Coco, but both Maggie and Cooper rushed to her, Maggie reaching her first. Guy kept his distance.

Cooper caught up with Maggie. "I've got this. She's *my* sister," he said. "Charlotte?" Cooper placed his hands on Charlotte's shoulders and turned her toward him. Sadie was surprised at the compassion in his voice. Maybe she'd pegged him wrong. Or maybe blood was thicker than disagreements.

Charlotte stopped sobbing and looked at Cooper as if she didn't recognize him for a second. "I can't believe she's gone, Coop. Sometimes I *hated* her *so* much, but I also *loved* her *so* much." She leaned against her brother's chest. He put his arms around her gingerly, as if he'd never hugged his sister before or hadn't hugged her in a long time.

"Why don't we follow Sadie's lead and go for a short walk?"

Charlotte wiped her eyes on her sleeve, nodded, and took his hand.

Every person in the room breathed a sigh of relief when the siblings left to go stroll in the orchard.

Elaine joined the two young men who were pulling items out of the boxes and stacking them on a table. "I *told* her the napkins would be here before six," she said. "Oh, Sadie, would you mind taste-testing something we plan to serve? I just made these Butterfinger Krispie Bars."

"Anything for the cause," Sadie offered eagerly. She took a bite, closed her eyes, and sighed. "Delicious."

"I think Dwight is in the ballroom," Maggie said. "I'll go see what he thinks we need to do next to get this event on track."

"I suppose we should go to the ballroom too," Sadie said to Guy. "Dwight will probably need to put both of us to work. If you're willing to help, that is."

"I'd be more than happy to help. It would give me a chance to…" Guy stopped himself. "Yes. I'd be more than happy to help."

Sadie stopped to retrieve the tote bag she'd left in a corner, unhooked Coco's leash, and settled her on the comfy cushion in the center. "Onward into the fray then," she said.

When they entered the ballroom, Sadie stopped short as a wave of dread washed over her. For a moment she was afraid she would see Roberta lying on the floor covered in crystals from the chandelier. But the chandelier was gone, of course. Guy was watching her closely.

"You can feel her energy in this room, can't you," he said.

Sadie glared at him. Something in his tone both unsettled and annoyed her. "I have no idea what you're talking about."

"Of course you don't." Guy smiled and strolled to the center of the space. The room was currently lit with wall sconces and a few standing lamps someone on the staff had brought in temporarily until they could replace the chandelier, which Sadie assumed would happen early the next morning. "I wonder if Roberta could sense the malevolent energy before the entity struck her down."

While Guy had grown on her, Sadie was feeling frustrated with his talk of spirits and energies and entities. "It wasn't an entity, Guy. It was a human being, an actual living murderer."

"Whatever you say." His smile disappeared.

Guy's height proved to be an advantage. Dwight put him to work on a ladder where he secured the tree branches to the wall areas surrounding the sconces. Sadie set about arranging ghoulish centerpieces for the tables. Maggie had vanished, but Sadie knew there were tasks to be done all over the property. It only made sense that she would float from one location to another.

As the work continued, the ballroom began, slowly, to transform from the horror show it had been at the beginning of the week into something like a Halloween version of the ballroom in the Cinderella story.

Sadie happened to turn toward the now open double doors and saw, to her secret delight, Broussard standing just outside. She hurried to him and looked up into his handsome but oddly serious face. "Detective Broussard! What are you doing here? Don't you and Froggy have some detecting to do?"

Broussard looked uncharacteristically uncomfortable. "I'm here with Frogert, and we are on police business. I'm sorry, Sadie." He turned away from her and walked over to the ladder where Guy was perched. "Mr. Bijou? I need to have a word with you."

Guy looked down, and Sadie thought for a moment that he might fall off the ladder. "Detective!" he said. "Of course you can have a word." He scrambled down the rungs quickly and stood before Broussard. "It's good to see you again." Guy glanced at Sadie. She could tell he was nervous because he was biting his lower lip.

"You may not think so in just a moment," Broussard mumbled. He took Guy's arm and guided him into the foyer where Sadie saw Froggy waiting.

"What's going on, Detectives?" Sadie asked as she stepped into the foyer.

"This doesn't concern you, Ms. Kramer," Frogert said. He pulled a pair of handcuffs from a back pocket and proceeded to place them around Guy's wrists. "Guy Bijou, I'm placing you under arrest..." Frogert continued to read Guy his Miranda rights as he guided him out the front door.

Sadie gasped and turned to Broussard. "What are you doing? Guy is perfectly harmless."

Broussard stared at Sadie and pointed to his forehead, which now sported a plain beige bandage. A flash of a thought ran through Sadie's head in spite of the seriousness of the situation: the bat bandage had been more appropriate for the holiday. Maybe she would find him another one.

"Surely you don't think that was *intentional*," Sadie said.

Broussard watched Froggy place Guy in the back of the squad car. He bent down so he could speak quietly to Sadie. "We need to ask Mr. Bijou some questions. It's better to do it out of the earshot of everyone here."

"But are you really arresting him?" Sadie tried to keep her voice low too.

"It appears so."

Just as Froggy was about to close the squad car's door, Guy called out to Sadie, "My hat! I left my hat in the ballroom!"

"I'll keep it for you," she called back. "You'll be back here in no time."

TWENTY-TWO

Sadie recovered Guy's hat and ran her fingers around its brim. What was Broussard thinking? Guy had been scared when Broussard chased him off the property. He wasn't dangerous or violent despite what Broussard and Froggy thought about Guy's show and what had happened on the set in New Orleans.

Something was going on that Sadie didn't quite understand. Things were going off the rails this afternoon, and she needed another quick break so she could think through some the possibilities and get away from the chaos. She was tempted to call Broussard to see what was going on with Guy, but she knew he would be unable to tell her.

She thought about grabbing Coco and making a run for it, going back to Flair, forgetting she'd ever offered to help Roberta and then Charlotte, and forgetting the Wainwright family entirely. The situation felt too heavy this afternoon. Maybe she should call it quits until tomorrow. No one was paying her to help, after all. She returned to the ballroom where she made sure Coco was still sleeping in the tote bag and not off destroying a bat decoration and gathered her up. When she turned to leave, she saw Seymour Wainwright standing in the doorway, looking perplexed and, Sadie thought, hopeful. His grayish hair was spiky, as if he'd been dragging his fingers through it.

"Did I just see the police detective put someone into his

car? Did they arrest someone for Roberta's murder?" He stared at Sadie, who held Guy's hat in one hand and her tote in the other. "They did arrest a man named Guy Bijou," she said. She didn't add anything more because she wasn't really sure *why* they'd arrested Guy.

Seymour stumbled into the ballroom and sat down hard on a chair. "Then it's over? They have him?"

Before she could answer, Charlotte and Cooper returned from their walk in the orchard and entered the ballroom where Seymour rested. Charlotte ran to him, knelt down, and put her arms around him.

"I'm so glad you're here, Daddy. It's been such a crazy day. A crazy week, in fact. I'm sorry I accused you of cheating on Mother when I didn't know all the circumstances."

Sadie blinked. *So they had it out then.*

Seymour stroked Charlotte's head. "It's all right, pumpkin, I understand. This is such a desperate and awful time for all of us."

Cooper gazed at Sadie and raised an eyebrow at the hat in her hand. "Are you off somewhere?"

"Emergency at my store. I need to rescue my assistant," she said. *No harm in a little white lie.*

"Well, go to it then." Cooper turned away abruptly, and Sadie bristled a bit. She didn't need his permission to do anything.

She nodded a curt goodbye and walked to the front of the mansion where she encountered Maggie.

"Are you leaving?" Maggie asked.

Sadie sighed. "Yes. I need to go back to Flair for a bit. Amber, my assistant, called, and she needs me to help with a tricky shipment and a recalcitrant printer. It's an emergency." *And no harm in polishing the little white lie a bit.*

"Of course! I don't know why I've forgotten that you have your own business to attend to," Maggie said. "What happened with Guy Bijou was pretty dramatic. Are you all right about that?"

"I have to be."

"I can tell you're fond of him. I imagine it's hard to see a friend arrested."

Sadie thought about that. Was Guy as close as a friend? She'd made friends with Myrtle pretty quickly, and now they communicated at least once a week.

"I haven't known Guy very long, but I admit he's grown on me. It's distressing to think he may be a killer."

Quietly, Maggie said, "I understand someone died on the set of his show last year, so maybe it's not so farfetched."

"Who told you that?"

"Cooper. He told me he liked to watch *Ghosts and Goblins* because of all the old houses they featured. He was disappointed when it went off the air for what the entertainment sites called a hiatus, so he did some digging and found out Guy was a 'person of interest' or something. But he was cleared of any wrongdoing, Cooper said." Maggie tucked her hair behind her right ear.

"I didn't realize you and Cooper were so friendly," Sadie said. She put the tote bag down next to her. This was not going to be a twenty-second chat.

"Cooper is friendly with everyone, as you might have been able to tell when he flirted with poor Elaine. But he's not a bad guy. In fact..." She looked over her shoulder to make sure no one was close enough to overhear. "I find a lot to admire about him. He's funny, cute, and lives life to the fullest. I think he's finally starting to discover that he *can* be ambitious."

"Really?" Since Sadie had met Cooper the day his mother

died, she hadn't been able to pin down his nature. Was he a loving son? A playboy? A beachcomber? A hardworking construction engineer? He'd been kind to Charlotte when she was in mid-meltdown, but was that just a show?

"Yes. He's been trying to convince the foundation board, and especially Roberta, that selling off the orchard part of the Wainwright property makes good sense and would not only increase the family's personal fortunes but would also add to the amount of money in the foundation's coffers."

"I did hear or read something about that," Sadie said. She thought about the discussion between Cooper and Keith Cross that she'd heard at the café.

"Roberta wasn't having it though. She was adamant that the estate be kept in one piece and not sold off piecemeal, as she called it. She also loved the trees and the gardens. She wouldn't budge."

Sadie stored that information in her mind and was about to ask another question when her cell phone buzzed. She bent down and dug it out of her tote and answered without looking at the number. "Excuse me," she said to Maggie. "I need to take this. Hello?"

"Ms. Kramer."

"Detective Broussard." Sadie was aware that her voice was chillier than normal. She glanced at Maggie, who waved and went back into the mansion, where Sadie hoped her cool head could help keep Charlotte calm. She also hoped any encounter Maggie had with Seymour wouldn't be awkward.

"I was wondering if you were free for dinner this evening," he said.

"Are you sure you want to have a meal with someone you don't trust?" Sadie knew she sounded snippy but couldn't help herself.

"What are you talking about?"

"Guy's arrest. Why didn't you tell me you were going to arrest him?"

"I couldn't," Broussard said, "and I still can't talk about it. But you know we, Frogert and I, wouldn't have taken this step if we didn't deem it absolutely necessary."

Sadie did know, and the thought of a leisurely and delicious meal with the detective was more appealing than staying home and sulking in her penthouse.

"All right. I give in. I'll pick you up at your hotel at seven."

"Perfect," he said and ended the call.

With Coco safely secured, Sadie sat in the driver's seat, thinking before she turned on the ignition. Where should she go, the penthouse or Flair? Flair had the advantage of Amber's willingness to listen and let her bounce ideas off her as well as close proximity to Matteo's chocolates. But the penthouse's luxurious bathroom, where she could soak in a bubble bath and contemplate the day, called to her.

"Come on, Coco, let's go home."

TWENTY-THREE

Sadie took a sip of wine and looked out at the bay from the waterside table at Fisherman's Wharf. The location had been an obvious choice for a nice dinner with Broussard. Not only was the view fabulous, the Dungeness Crab Cakes were divine.

"A perfect evening in spite of phone interruptions," Broussard said as he slid back into the seat across from Sadie. She appreciated the fact he'd taken the call outside instead of talking right at the table. She'd seen this trend lately and sometimes wondered if anyone had good manners anymore. Obviously, Broussard did. Just another thing she liked about him.

"I take it that was Froggy," Sadie said, instantly wondering if she was being too nosy. He'd certainly offer that information on his own if he wanted to.

"Yes," he replied immediately, to Sadie's relief. "He's checking some files I sent him on the *Ghosts and Goblins* accident in New Orleans."

"So you suspect Guy? That's why you arrested him?"

"We suspect everyone until we rule people out. That's our job. If we don't stay objective, we could overlook crucial clues. We have our reasons for arresting Guy, and I can only tell you, the arrest involved his television program."

Sadie tilted her head inquisitively and smiled, surprised at the rather coquettish move on her part. "Well, if you suspect everyone, then am I a suspect?" She picked up her glass of chardonnay and took another sip while waiting for the obvious answer.

Broussard laughed. "I wouldn't worry about that. You were ruled out pretty quickly. Though Frogert did suggest it..."

"What?" Sadie almost spit out her wine.

Broussard laughed even louder this time, enough to turn a few heads at nearby tables. "Not seriously, my dear amateur detective. But you have to admit you show up at a lot of scenes like this."

"Pure coincidence," Sadie said. "Or bad luck. Or some of each, I suppose." She set her wine down and leaned forward, lowering her voice. "So you two really think Guy is guilty? I don't believe it."

"You know I can't comment on an ongoing investigation."

"Even to me?" Sadie tried the tilted head smile again. It couldn't hurt. The gesture felt less sincere in view of her worries for Guy.

"Even to you."

"Well then, I'll tell you what I think from my own investigating." Sadie's copper bangles clunked against the table as she leaned forward, eager to discuss the case. Broussard chuckled, and Sadie raised an eyebrow. "What's so funny?"

"I think you might have missed your calling, my dear," Broussard said.

"Perhaps," Sadie mused. "I do enjoy trying to solve these puzzles."

"Then I assure you that you *didn't* miss your calling. Because these puzzles, as you call them, are better known as hard and often frustrating work when you do them all the time."

"I can see that." Sadie selected a slice of warm sourdough from a basket in the center of the table. She buttered the bread and then poked at the air with it as she spoke, almost like an orchestra conductor directing a staccato passage. "I've had a couple of interesting conversations with Maggie today."

"And?"

"I stopped by her office before I went to the mansion, and I asked her about the note from Seymour, the one that Charlotte found and gave me to pass on to Froggy. I'm guessing you know about the note."

"Yes," Broussard said. "In which Seymour professes his feelings for Maggie but says he plans to stay with Roberta."

"Maggie, however, could have been swayed by the note," Sadie said, thinking out loud. "So she could be with Seymour, right?" Sadie watched for Broussard's reaction and got the one she'd expected.

"It's possible," Broussard said evasively.

"Well, it only makes sense. He made it clear Roberta was the only thing standing in the way of them being together. Unless..." Sadie drummed her fingertips on the tabletop. "Unless she didn't *want* to be with Seymour. She did tell me she's in love with someone else."

Broussard raised his eyebrows. "Really? Well, that's quite interesting."

"I thought so," Sadie said. "Because it takes her motive away."

"*If* she's telling the truth," Broussard pointed out. "It could also be a clever cover story. You'd be surprised what people come up with to deflect attention."

"I suppose so," Sadie said. "Maybe she really *is* in love with Seymour and just wanted to throw me off, knowing I'd be talking to Froggy."

"Exactly," Broussard said. "However, in this case you may be right about Maggie being in love with someone else."

"And why is that?" Sadie examined a forkful of crab cake and then took a bite.

"Because, according to Frogert, Cooper is in love with Maggie."

"Well!" Sadie almost dropped her fork. "I didn't see that coming."

"You didn't hear it from me. And I didn't hear it from Frogert."

"I see," Sadie said. "Thank goodness for so many things not being heard by so many people. So we have a little love mixed into the Wainwright drama?"

"More like a love *triangle*," Broussard pointed out. "Which is another scenario altogether."

"Maggie, Seymour, and Cooper? Interesting." Sadie contemplated that. "Seymour is much older than Maggie, but he certainly isn't the first man to be interested in a younger woman. And from Maggie's viewpoint…"

"Money," Broussard said. "And Seymour is…"

"Loaded," Sadie said. *No point in understating the obvious.*

"Yes. Very."

Sadie nodded. "A solid motive for a love interest."

"Yet there's a wife in the way," Broussard said. "Getting rid of the wife would give access to the man and the money. Hypothetically, of course."

"Cooper and Maggie are closer in age," Sadie said. "She's what, only four or five years older than he is? She didn't name the person she's in love with, but it certainly sounds like it could be Cooper."

"Unless she's lying."

"To cover up the fact she's after Seymour and his money."

"Or simply the money," Broussard said. "Seymour could just be the stepping stone. Sorry to say it, but this job can make a person cynical. We don't always see the best in people."

"If you did, you probably wouldn't solve many cases," Sadie pointed out.

"You have a good point there. What else did you learn from Maggie?"

Sadie thought about both the conversations she'd had with Maggie earlier that day. "Well, this isn't so much something that Maggie told me, but when I visited her at the foundation offices, she had this mask she was playing with while we spoke, a lovely glittering mask that reminded me of the one…" She couldn't continue.

Broussard covered her free hand. "It's all right. You don't have to say it. Did you find out where she got the mask?"

"Yes, she said Seymour gave it to her last week and suggested she wear it to the Spooktacular."

"Interesting." Broussard speared a cherry tomato and popped it into his mouth.

"What about Cooper?" Sadie hoped a casual drop of Cooper's name might pry a little more information out of Broussard.

"What about him?"

So much for that. "He seems preoccupied with all his business deals. He's not very involved with the mansion or the foundation except for helping to pull together the Spooktacular every year, from what I can tell."

"I can't get into specifics," Broussard reminded Sadie. "But I would… guess that Cooper has some big development projects up in the air."

"Right," Sadie said. "The sale of the orchard half of the property."

Broussard said nothing.

"He and a reporter, Keith Cross, happened to be at the

café the morning I gave Froggy Seymour's love letter, and I overheard them talking about the possible sale."

"You seem to gather a lot of data when you're around coffee," Broussard said, but he didn't go into the details Sadie hoped he would.

"And…" Sadie tried to see inside what Broussard was not saying. Guessing and interpreting his reaction was her best option at this point. "And other deals… that depend on… the sale of the orchard to finance!" Pleased with this connection, she rewarded herself with another slice of sourdough.

"It's quite possible," Broussard said. "Hypothetically, of course. One business deal often hinges on another."

"And since Roberta was adamantly against the sale of the orchard, this could cause him to lose the other deals."

"That's my understanding."

"Maggie mentioned that Roberta wouldn't budge on this issue." Sadie thought back. "Cooper told me the first time I spoke with him that his mother was coming around to seeing things his way. But he could easily have been lying if he knew she wouldn't be able to contradict him."

"Lying is always a possibility in this type of situation."

"And Charlotte?" Sadie asked. She thought about Charlotte's near rage while everyone worked toward getting the mansion ready for the weekend's gala. And she wondered suddenly about Dwight's car keys, how Charlotte seemed to be the only person in the kitchen who knew where they could be found.

Broussard looked a little surprised. "Charlotte Wainwright? Frogert said when he interviewed her, she seemed like a doting daughter with nothing to hide, and he didn't turn up anything other than her job, which apparently she does very well. Did you hear something?"

"Another thing from Maggie. Apparently Roberta kept

threatening to decrease Charlotte's inheritance. But Maggie didn't know much about the Wainwrights' living trust or wills, so she wasn't sure if the threat held water."

Broussard rubbed his chin. "I'll pass that along to Frogert. You are just a fount of information, Ms. Kramer. Don't hold back."

Sadie brushed a few bread crumbs on the table into a small pile as she thought. "One thing I forgot to tell you *or* Froggy has to do with the chandelier. I was so focused on Seymour's note to Maggie that it just flew out of my brain."

"Explain," Broussard said.

"The first day I helped with the Spooktacular setup, I met Dwight, the mansion caretaker, and he talked about how he often shows the Wainwrights all about the building's unique features."

"And this includes the chandelier?" Broussard asked.

"Yes. He taught Cooper, Seymour, and even Charlotte how to operate the mechanism a few months ago, though Charlotte said she thought the dumbwaiter was cooler," Sadie said. "Can you remember all these things, Detective?"

Broussard tapped his temple. "It's all up here, my dear."

"But what do you make of all these pieces?" Sadie asked.

"They make a pretty scrambled puzzle."

"So they're all still suspects," Sadie said, feeling they were no closer to an answer than they had been the day before.

"For now," Broussard said. "But we're getting close." Broussard folded his napkin and set it on the table. "What do you say we go off in search of some chocolate and a cable car ride?"

"Ah, you've uttered the magic word." Sadie stood up and looped her tote bag straps over her shoulder.

"Cable or car?"

"Very funny," Sadie said. "Fortunately, both your suggestions are within walking distance. But we must have priorities. Ghirardelli Square, here we come."

TWENTY-FOUR

Nervous energy buzzed throughout the mansion and grounds in a way not untypical for tech rehearsals of any kind. There was always a sense that something was bound to go wrong before a big event even if no one had any idea what it would be. An electrical circuit could blow a fuse not readily available to replace, a rental company might deliver the wrong chairs and tables, or a pipe might burst, leaving the caterers without use of the kitchen. The hope was always that it would go wrong at the rehearsal, not at the event itself.

Sadie arrived just as Charlotte was briskly traversing the back garden, waving her arms this way and that. Two men in work clothes trailed behind her as she pointed to one location after another. Following her directions, they marked off seating areas to accommodate groups in size from two to twenty. Once the overall plan was set, they headed to a large rental equipment truck parked behind the garden and proceeded to unload stacks of chairs and small tables.

"Here to help?"

The sound of Cooper's voice took Sadie by surprise, as she hadn't heard him approach. She turned to find him standing beside her with an expression that struck her as smug. She nodded. "Why not? It's been a tough week for you all. I'm sure Charlotte can use the extra support."

Cooper cleared his throat. "Charlotte may be high-strung,

but as you could see yesterday, she has a way of getting people to do what she needs. It's not Mother's way of operating, but she's quite adept at making things go her way." He stuck his hands in his pockets and rocked back on his heels. "The Spooktacular will be perfect. Mother liked to be in charge of everything too, but she handled it a little bit better. Still, her bossiness was very annoying."

Sadie thought about Roberta's panicked phone the morning she died and wondered if that were true. Maybe Cooper didn't know his mother as well as he thought.

"I guess that's how things get done," Sadie said, half in support of Charlotte and Roberta, and half for lack of anything else to say. Cooper seemed to have a surly attitude at the moment, and Sadie doubted countering anything he said would be a smart move. "In any case, I did promise your mother I would help."

"Yes," Cooper said. "And you've certainly been helping a lot this week. Every day."

Sadie bit her tongue, not sure how to interpret his comment. Did he think she hadn't done enough? She *had* been helping. Hadn't she arranged the fake tombstones on the front lawn to his satisfaction? Or helped Dwight and Elaine with the buffet arrangement when Cooper was too busy with a real estate phone call to lend a hand? Or was he implying she'd been helping Froggy and Broussard a bit too much and the Wainwright family not enough? Or had someone else come along to block the sale of the orchard?

"Where's your detective buddy?" Cooper checked his phone for messages, and Sadie found herself wondering if he ever put it down. She could envision him sleeping with his hand wrapped around it. Even though Cooper seemed like a pretty laid-back person, maybe the business dealings he was trying to close were making him as high-strung as his sister.

"Busy detecting, I imagine," Sadie quipped. *On his way here, Cooper.* "I'm going inside to see if they have the ballroom lights set. I'm eager to see the new chandelier."

Cooper relaxed and smiled. "You'll see that it looks great. I've pretty much become an chandelier aficionado after all the old houses I've sold. You go ahead. I'm going to wait outside for Dad. He should be here any minute." He turned to face the street, and Sadie headed into the mansion.

Dwight was perched once again on a ladder when Sadie entered, troubleshooting one track of twisted branches with tiny bulbs that weren't lighting up though all the others were working. Maggie hovered around a giant cauldron-shaped punch bowl that sat inside an even bigger cauldron, helping Elaine arrange burnt orange and yellow leaves around the base.

"I see the punch bowl is here," Sadie said. "Er, bowls, plural, it appears."

"Thank goodness," Maggie said. "One less thing for Charlotte to worry about. Though she is calmer tonight."

"Slightly," Elaine added, rolling her eyes. She stepped back, inspected the table arrangement, and then returned to adjust the leaves.

Sadie leaned forward and inspected the sizable moat between the two cauldron-shaped punch bowls. Coco popped up over the edge of the tote bag and appeared to do the same.

"Dry ice," Elaine explained. "It'll go between the two bowls to make it look like steam is rising from them.

"How clever!" Sadie said. "I've always wondered how that works."

"How what works?"

Sadie looked up to see Broussard had arrived. His expression struck her as surprisingly official though he greeted her with a smile. "The steam around a witch's cauldron," she said. "They put dry ice between two bowls. It looks so real."

"Things are not always what they seem," Broussard said. "Do you think anyone could use my help?" he asked.

Sadie nodded. "Dwight can always use some assistance." She pointed across the room to where the caretaker was just climbing down from the ladder, the tiny lights on the branches now working properly.

"Excuse me then." Broussard left Sadie and joined the caretaker, and the two men moved to the side exit of the ballroom where Broussard held the ladder as Dwight checked the wiring behind a speaker above the door.

Charlotte swept into and across the room.

"Oh, Elaine, the table looks fantastic!"

"And the punch bowls are even here," Elaine whispered to Sadie, who laughed and then excused herself as she saw Froggy enter. Guy followed just behind, his hands behind his back. Sadie joined the two of them near the ballroom entrance. As she expected, Guy's appearance earned a quick reaction.

"What is he doing here?" Seymour's voice boomed out above the others, drawing stares from all directions. "He killed my wife!"

"I don't think so," Sadie said. She glanced at Froggy, who nodded permission for her to go ahead. "But the killer is here in this room."

Charlotte crossed her arms. "That's ridiculous." She glanced around, and Sadie glimpsed a momentary return of the frazzled daughter present the past few days. "We all loved Mother."

Some more than others, Sadie mused.

"Absolutely," Cooper echoed. Phone in hand, his arm dropped to his side. "What's the meaning of this? You arrested this man yesterday for our mother's murder. He should be in jail!"

"We're family!" Charlotte cried. "We'd never hurt each other." She and Cooper exchanged worried glances. "You can't possibly be accusing us."

"That's right," Seymour shouted. "This is preposterous! Take that man back to jail right now! Charlotte and Cooper would never hurt their mother."

Sadie reached behind Guy's back and pulled a tripod out, a clunky metal object attached to the top. Guy's arms relaxed by his side. She held it out and addressed Seymour. "Did you really think Guy would use this type of amateur equipment? A beginner level ghost-tracker?"

Seymour's angry expression faltered, and he took a step back. "I've never seen that before. I don't even know what it is."

Guy spoke up. "It's an EMF tracker. It measures electromagnetic frequencies. And Sadie is correct. I wouldn't use this one. My equipment is far more expensive and far more sophisticated. I'm a professional paranormal investigator, after all." He held his head up proudly. Froggy coughed.

"This is what you used to kill Roberta," Sadie said. "You hit her over the head with it, then dropped the chandelier on her to make it look just like the incident where Amelia Wainwright died in 1925, glittering mask and all. Guy told me the story." Sadie heard someone gasp and realized it was Maggie. "Then you hid the tripod and meter in the orchard on your way out, hoping it would implicate Guy when the police found it. Detective Broussard discovered it in some bushes and noticed the blood on the meter."

"This is ridiculous," Seymour sputtered. "Everyone knows I was out of town. I have my plane ticket to prove it."

"But were you really away?" Sadie asked. She nodded to Froggy.

Froggy stepped forward and pulled a paper from his front pocket. "I have the airline records to show you never got on that plane."

"You drove your car to the airport the day your plane was supposed to depart and left it in long-term parking, then took an Uber back into town where you hid out in your office for a night," Sadie said. "You took another Uber to the mansion late the morning of Roberta's death."

"You're crazy!" Seymour snarled. "The airlines are mistaken!"

"You'd been planning this for months," Sadie said. "You knew about the accident on Guy's show and lured him up here for the Spooktacular under the guise of wanting publicity. You played on his hopes to get the show back on the air. You knew if he was here in San Francisco when Roberta died, because of what happened before, he would look suspicious."

"You set me up," Guy said.

"Daddy, tell me this isn't true!" Charlotte's eyes filled with tears, and she began to crumble to the floor. Cooper caught her before she fell.

"But why, Dad," Cooper asked over his sister's head. "Why on earth would you murder Mom? What did she ever do to you but make you look good in the eyes of the community? She worked hard for you, harder than either of us." Cooper gestured to Charlotte.

Seymour looked at Maggie, who was standing next to Elaine, shocked. "I did it for me and Maggie, so we could be together the way we wanted to be."

"Oh, Seymour! You didn't!" Maggie cried. "I told you I was in love with someone else. I've never been in love with you."

Seymour took a step back. "That can't be true. Who do you love?"

Maggie moved toward Cooper and Charlotte. "I love your son. I'm in love with Cooper."

"You are?" Cooper said.

Maggie touched her fingers to Cooper's cheek. "I am."

Seymour took one more step back, turned, and bolted for the side door. Broussard tackled him as Dwight blocked the exit. Both Seymour and Broussard fell to the floor in the struggle. Finally Seymour gave up and looked at Maggie. "I truly believed you loved me," he said.

Maggie shook her head mutely and held on to Cooper's arm. His head swiveled between Seymour and Maggie, and Sadie thought for a moment he might combust from the mixed emotions of discovering simultaneously that Maggie loved him and that his father murdered his mother.

"I'll take it from here," Froggy said. He had crossed the ballroom during the attempted escape. He cuffed Seymour and read him his rights. As Froggy led him out of the mansion, Seymour called over his shoulder. "I'm sorry, Charlotte! I'm sorry, Cooper!"

"Let's go." Froggy pushed him toward the mansion's grand entrance.

"The Broussard Tackle is getting lots of use," Sadie said to the detective as he rubbed his forehead. The wound from his confrontation with Guy in the orchard had broken open again. With her usual impeccable timing, Coco popped up from inside the tote bag with a strip of paper in her mouth.

"Thank you, Coco," Sadie said as she took the flimsy strip. She turned to Broussard and reached out with the offering. "Bat bandage?"

TWENTY-FIVE

Sadie stepped out of her car, took one look at the scene in front of her, and caught her breath. The Wainwright mansion was like something out of a fairy tale. Haunted, perhaps, but enchanting all the same. The pumpkin luminaries that lined the front walkway cast a magical spell. Tiny twinkling lights wrapped around the columns and banisters of the front porch, beckoning as if a castle waiting for its prince and princess to arrive. Each window of the second and third floors echoed the sparkling lights below, outlining silhouettes of ghosts in a way that appeared more whimsical than scary. Sadie wasn't sure she'd ever seen a vision this lovely before, certainly not at Halloween.

Broussard stepped beside her, and she slipped her hand into the crook of his elbow, delighting in the sense of security she felt. It had been a long time since she'd stood side by side with a partner. And although their relationship was as yet undefined, she had a strong feeling that things were headed that way. Partners. It had a nice ring to it.

"Shall we, Ms. Kramer?" Broussard extended his free arm forward to suggest a walk up to the front entrance where steel pumpkins from a local metalwork artist graced each marble step. An orange glow from inside each creation wove its way through long sculpted slits, combining to create flickering waves of luminescence across the marble staircase.

"I think we shall, Detective Broussard," Sadie said, eager

to enter the mansion and let the warm ambiance wash away the hard work, stress, and emotions of the past week. She smoothed the red dress she'd picked up at the dry cleaners, pleased with her Lady in Red costume choice. Glancing at Broussard as they approached the stairs, she could hardly believe he'd managed to secure a tux rental, complete with top hat. To say he looked handsome would be an understatement. And together, the mix of red, black, and white was impressive.

The inside of the mansion looked every bit as wonderful as it had at the tech rehearsal, even better without the drama of the night before to dampen the mood. Champagne bubbled from glasses held by pirates, witches, mermaids, and princesses alike. Sadie was certain she saw Marie Antoinette exchange laughter with Marilyn Monroe just beside the ballroom door.

"There you are!" Charlotte, dressed as a flamenco dancer, raced up to Sadie. Castanets clattered against each other as they dangled from a ribbon around her wrist. She gave Broussard a pleading look. "You must let me steal her for a moment, Detective."

"By all means," Broussard said. "I'm going to mosey over to say hello to Charlie Chaplin and his wife."

"Which one?" Sadie asked, her eyes following the direction of Broussard's nod. "He was married four times, you know."

"Indeed, that's true," Charlotte said. "I have a hunch the one you'll find him with tonight is Oona O'Neill, the playwright Eugene O'Neill's daughter."

"How did you know that?" Sadie asked once Charlotte had pulled her away. "I mean, how did you know which wife?"

Charlotte laughed. "Because I spoke with Detective Frogert and his wife, Oona, as soon as they arrived."

"Oh my," Sadie exclaimed. "Charlie Chaplin is Froggy? This I have to see!"

"You definitely do. But first you *must* see the ballroom. The work crew did the most amazing job!" Charlotte grabbed Sadie's hand and guided her across the foyer, stopping to say hello to guests along the way.

Sadie looked up in wonder at the transformation of the ballroom ceiling. The chandelier from the drawing room, in spite of being slightly smaller than the previous ballroom's fixture, sparkled in its new location. Each crystal sent rays of reflected light to the others, creating a magical effect. "It's exquisite!" Sadie exclaimed.

"I wholeheartedly agree," Charlotte said. "Even more splendid than the other one, don't you think? Now that I'm seeing this, I think we'll just leave it here and order something different for the drawing room. In fact, maybe we'll do some additional redecorating. Restoration is more like it, preservation and such."

Sadie was thankful for Charlotte's continued chatter, which allowed her to avoid the question about the chandelier. Agreeing that it was nicer would have been an empty statement. After all, she'd only seen the other one on Roberta's head. Then again, all things considered, this certainly was nicer than *that* had been.

"Oh, I need to say hi to those people," Charlotte said, gesturing to a couple sipping champagne not far away. "Wander around, enjoy!" With that she flitted off in a rush.

Sadie considered a butterfly costume might have been more appropriate than the one she wore, but she was just happy that Charlotte had the necessary adrenaline to make it through the evening. She'd worked so hard to make this a success for her mother's memory. A difficult grieving period would certainly follow once the event was over.

Sadie glanced over at the ballroom wall and spied Guy and

Dwight. She laughed at the sight of their *Ghostbusters* attire. How quickly they'd made peace with each other and even managed to pull off matching costumes after all the times Dwight had run Guy off the property. She sent a thumbs-up to Guy, a gesture of congratulations for his show being picked up again after he emailed a pitch for a "Wainwright Mansion" episode.

Broussard caught up with Sadie, and they started to make the rounds of the ballroom. Their first stop was at the large black cauldron, foggy steam creeping upward from around its rim. Elaine, dressed similarly to Broussard, poured blood-red punch from a ladle shaped like a gnarled hand. Sadie eyed the beverage suspiciously before taking a sip. Pleased to find it tasted far less frightening than she'd feared, she clinked glasses with Broussard in a toast, and the two continued around the room.

"Aren't the musicians fabulous?" Sadie looked to Broussard for a response, and he nodded. "This overture to *Phantom of the Opera* is giving me chills. I never would have thought it possible to bring an organ in."

"I suppose anything is possible with the right budget. As they say, it takes money to make money, and they're certainly making some tonight."

"No doubt about that," Sadie said. "Tickets for this were two hundred fifty apiece, and there must be five hundred people here, counting those in the garden and orchard."

"Six figures," Broussard mused. "No wonder they didn't want to cancel it."

"So, Detective Broussard, what made you and Froggy realize Seymour Wainwright was the killer? The others had some pretty strong motives," Sadie said.

"Yes, they did," Broussard said. "Even before we figured out

Seymour hadn't really gone out of town, we started looking more deeply into his situation and character." He paused a little too long for Sadie's liking.

"Go on." She slowed down long enough to grab a Butterfinger Krispie Bar off a dessert platter.

"Frogert and I strongly suspected Cooper since he'd been pushing Mrs. Wainwright to sell the property to developers. We really thought he was desperate to get enough money to invest in other properties or even some kind of scheme since get-rich-quick schemes turned up when we investigated his past. But we found nothing that would implicate him. And he had an alibi for the time of his mother's murder. He met with a developer between the time he dropped Mrs. Wainwright off at the mansion and the time he returned to pick her up for lunch."

"All right." Sadie bit into the sweet treat and waited for Broussard to continue.

"We started looking into the Wainwrights' personal financials and Mrs. Wainwright's will. It turns out that while the Wainwright property had been in Seymour's family for generations, Roberta came into the marriage quite rich on her own."

Sadie frowned. "But everyone knows that Roberta was an heiress and wealthy in her own right."

"Ah, yes, but not everyone knows that Roberta was in the process of changing her will to leave her own estate to her children and directly to the foundation. She was going to write Seymour out entirely. He found out somehow."

Sadie led Broussard to a table. "I think I need to sit down for a minute. How in the world did you discover this?"

Broussard leaned close to Sadie's ear and whispered, "Because I'm the real detective here. Ouch," he added as Sadie elbowed him playfully.

"Roberta must have known Seymour was infatuated with Maggie," Sadie said. "Poor woman."

Amber, Dylan, and Matteo joined them, dressed as a hippie, rock star, and chef, respectively.

"I dropped the large platter of truffles Roberta ordered off to Elaine," Matteo said.

"It was awesome of Charlotte to allow you to invite us," Dylan offered.

"She's actually quite a lovely person when you get to know her," Sadie said. She introduced the trio of friends to Broussard.

"I'm so glad to finally meet you," Amber said. "Sadie talks about you a lot." She ignored a shy hush from her employer. "I actually thought it might be Charlotte who was the guilty one on this case. After Sadie told me about the threat to cut her inheritance."

"We looked into that," Charlie Chaplin said, overhearing Amber as he joined them. "It turns out it was an empty threat Roberta used all the time, a kind of reminder to her daughter that she had all the power. According to her attorney, she never intended to reduce Charlotte's inheritance."

"Why, Detective Frogert!" Amber exclaimed. "You look fantastic."

Froggy stepped back just far enough to safely twirl his cane. The woman dressed as Oona Chaplin stood smiling as she watched. He put his arm around her shoulder. "This is my lovely wife, Oona Frogert."

Sadie motioned toward the refreshment table, suggesting Amber, Dylan, and Matteo follow. "Come with me. I'll introduce you to the most patient caterer in all of San Francisco. You can have some extremely frightening punch while we're at it."

"And a few truffles," Matteo suggested, a tip they eagerly accepted.

After an exchange of greetings next to the foggy punch cauldron, Dylan turned to Amber. "I overheard someone say 'Thriller' was playing on the sound system in the orchard. Care to go dance with some zombies?" Amber enthusiastically agreed.

"Ah, to be young again." Sadie sighed, contentedly watching the couple head outside.

"We're as young as we feel," Broussard said, slipping his arm around Sadie's waist. "And I do feel young tonight, thanks to this enchanting scenario." His gaze circled the room and then settled on Sadie. "And equally enchanting company, I might add." Leaning toward her, he placed a sweet kiss on her forehead, one that promised more to come.

"Well, well. Look at this handsome couple," Cooper Wainwright said as he and Maggie approached Sadie and Broussard. He clung to Maggie's hand and managed to look both obnoxiously pleased with himself and like a little boy who couldn't believe his luck. Maggie was dressed as an angel with a pair of bright blue wings strapped across her back over a long, flowing light-blue robe. Cooper was dressed in black slacks, a black turtleneck, and black shoes. He had a daub of black theatre makeup on each cheek and carried a ski mask in one hand.

"What are you supposed to be?" Sadie asked.

"A jewel thief."

Maggie laughed. She drew close to Sadie and said quietly, "I think I could die of happiness tonight."

The older couple watched the younger couple leave to dance in the garden. Sadie spotted a familiar figure at the entrance to the ballroom. "Look, Detective, it's my snooping reporter friend, Keith Cross." She pulled Broussard behind her. "I feel like I might need to protect him from Froggy. He is *not* a fan of this boy."

Keith looked a little overwhelmed as he surveyed the grandeur and magic of the room. When he noticed Sadie, he smiled broadly. "Hello, Ms. Kramer."

"Hello Mr. Cross. This is my friend, Detective Broussard." The two men shook hands. "Do the Wainwrights know you're here?"

"I think so. I was invited to cover this extravaganza by someone named Guy Bijou."

Ah, Sadie thought, *a male who doesn't watch* Guy's Ghosts and Goblins. *He must be too busy doing his own investigations.*

Keith caught sight of Charlotte flitting through the crowd. "Is that the Wainwright daughter?"

"Yes," Sadie said.

"She's, er…" He stopped.

"Stunning?" Sadie suggested. "Why don't you go ask her to dance?"

He took a step toward Charlotte and nodded to Sadie and Broussard.

"Why do I feel like you've shifted your new calling from amateur detective to matchmaker?" Broussard asked.

Sadie shrugged. "I have no idea what you're talking about."

Coco popped up from the center of the tote and barked three times. She wore a red ribbon that matched Sadie's dress on her head.

"Oh, yes, you do," Broussard said.

Little by little, as the evening progressed, the crowd thinned until only the Wainwright siblings, Sadie, and Broussard remained.

"Would you like us to help clean up?" Sadie offered the

exhausted brother and sister. Both Charlotte and Cooper shook their heads.

"Absolutely not," Charlotte said. "Dwight will be here tomorrow to take down the outside decorations and sound system. And Elaine and Maggie will handle the inside."

"I'll help with the inside too," Cooper said.

"And we've hired a crew to do the heavy work," Charlotte added. "You two were our guests this evening."

"Thank you for everything," Cooper said. "If it weren't for you, I'm not sure I would have found out how Maggie felt." He shook Broussard's hand and surprised Sadie by kissing her cheek. The interior lights began to turn off one by one. "I think that's Dwight's hint that it's time for us all to go. He'll make sure the mansion is secure and locked up."

All four stepped outside and said good night. Cooper escorted Charlotte to the Jaguar, which waited in front. Sadie pulled her keys from her tote bag.

As she and Broussard headed to her car, she glanced back and thought for a moment she could see the dangling crystals of the chandelier shaking as moonlight flowed in from outside. She pulled on Broussard's sleeve. "Look! Do you see that?"

Broussard turned back toward the mansion. "I don't see anything. What is it?"

Looking again, Sadie realized the chandelier and crystals were motionless and still. "Nothing, I guess. Just my imagination." She opened the car door for Broussard and circled around to the driver side. Once inside, she turned the ignition on. *Ghosts, goblins, and haunted chandeliers. Yes, just my imagination.*

Broussard reached over and squeezed her shoulder. "Enough excitement to last for a while, my dear amateur detective?"

"Absolutely!" Sadie said as she pulled away from the curb. *At least until next time.*

BUTTERFINGER KRISPIE BARS

(FROM KIM DAVIS OF *CINNAMON AND SUGAR AND A LITTLE BIT OF MURDER*)

A delicious way to use up Halloween candy

Ingredients
- 1 cup sugar
- 1 cup light corn syrup
- 1-1/2 cups peanut butter (creamy or crunchy)
- 6 cups (12 ounce box) Rice Krispies
- 1 12-ounce bag semi-sweet chocolate chips
- 1 12-ounce bag butterscotch chips
- 3 Butterfinger candy bars, crushed

Instructions
1. Line a jelly roll pan (12" x 18") with foil and spritz with non-stick cooking spray. Arrange the Rice Krispies over the bottom of the pan.
2. In a medium saucepan, stir together over low heat, sugar, corn syrup, and peanut butter.
3. Once the mixture has melted and is smooth, pour over the Rice Krispies. Stir until all the cereal is coated and pat flat onto the pan.
4. Place the chocolate chips and butterscotch chips together in a microwave-safe bowl. Heat in 30 second increments, stirring after each cycle, until melted. Spread over the Rice Krispies mixtures.
5. Before the chocolate/butterscotch spread sets, sprinkle with the Butterfinger crumbles.
6. Cut into bars while still warm, leaving them in the pan. Refrigerate for at least 30 minutes until firm and chocolate/butterscotch spread has set before serving.

Acknowledgments

A fictional tale only becomes a novel with the help of many people along the way. A Flair for Goblins, in particular, only exists because of extraordinary developmental editing by Elizabeth Christy. Her talent for plot contributions, character refinement, and scene structure laid the path for this story to come together.

Annie Sarac at The Editing Pen did a fabulous job polishing up the rough edges of the manuscript. The colorful covers that grace all the Sadie Kramer Flair Mysteries are thanks to Keri Knutson of Alchemy Book Covers and Design. Formatting credit goes to Tara Meyers and Kelly Gaffney. Jay Garner and Karen Putnam are due a round of applause for beta reading and feedback. And a very patient Paul Sterrett deserves at least a few days of reprieve from listening to me wander around debating plot points with anyone or anything—humans, canines, or even, at times, plants—that would listen.

The delicious recipe for Butterfinger Krispie Bars is courtesy of Kim Davis at Cinnamon and Sugar and a Little Bit of Murder. A culinary treasure trove of recipes can be found on her website: cinnamonsugarandalittlebitofmurder.com

As always, I'm grateful for the amazing support of family, friends, and readers. Their encouragement is what allows Sadie and Coco to enjoy a world of mystery.

Books by Deborah Garner

The Paige MacKenzie Series

Above the Bridge

When NY reporter Paige MacKenzie arrives in Jackson Hole, it's not long before her instincts tell her there's more than a basic story to be found in the popular, northwestern Wyoming mountain area. A chance encounter with attractive cowboy Jake Norris soon has Paige chasing a legend of buried treasure passed down through generations. Side- stepping a few shady characters who are also searching for the same hidden reward, she will have to decide who is trustworthy and who is not.

The Moonglow Café

The discovery of an old diary inside the wall of the historic hotel soon sends NY reporter Paige MacKenzie into the underworld of art and deception. Each of the town's residents holds a key to untangling more than one long-buried secret, from the hippie chick owner of a new age café to the mute homeless man in the town park. As the worlds of western art and sapphire mining collide, Paige finds herself juggling research, romance, and danger.

Three Silver Doves

The New Mexico resort of Agua Encantada seems a perfect destination for reporter Paige MacKenzie to combine work with well-deserved rest and relaxation. But when suspicious jewelry shows up on another guest, and the town's storyteller goes missing, Paige's R&R is soon redefined as restlessness and risk. Will an unexpected overnight trip to Tierra Roja Casino lead her to the answers she seeks, or are darker secrets lurking along the way?

Hutchins Creek Cache

When a mysterious 1920's coin is discovered behind the Hutchins Creek Railroad Museum in Colorado, Paige MacKenzie starts digging into four generations of Hutchins family history, with a little help from the Denver Mint. As legends of steam engines and coin mintage mingle, will Paige discover the true origin of the coin, or will she find herself riding the rails dangerously close to more than one long-hidden town secret?

Crazy Fox Ranch

As Paige MacKenzie returns to Jackson Hole, she has only two things on her mind: enjoy life with Wyoming's breathtaking Grand Tetons as the backdrop, and spend more time with handsome cowboy Jake Norris as he prepares to open his guest ranch. But when a stranger's odd behavior leads her to research western filming in the area—in particular, the movie *Shane*, will it simply lead to a freelance article for the *Manhattan Post*, or will it lead to a dangerous hidden secret?

The Sadie Kramer Flair Series

A Flair for Chardonnay

When flamboyant senior sleuth Sadie Kramer learns the owner of her favorite chocolate shop is in trouble, she heads for the California wine country with a tote-bagged Yorkie and a slew of questions. The fourth-generation Tremiato Winery promises answers, but not before a dead body turns up at the vintners' scheduled Harvest Festival. As Sadie juggles truffles, tips, and turmoil, she'll need to sort the grapes from the wrath in order to find the identity of the killer.

A Flair for Drama

When a former schoolmate invites Sadie Kramer to a theatre production, she jumps at the excuse to visit the Monterey Bay area for a weekend. Plenty of action is expected on stage, but when the show's leading lady turns up dead, Sadie finds herself faced with more than one drama to follow. With both cast members and production crew as potential suspects, will Sadie and her sidekick Yorkie, Coco, be able to solve the case?

A Flair for Beignets

With fabulous music, exquisite cuisine, and rich culture, how could a week in New Orleans be anything less than fantastic for Sadie Kramer and her sidekick Yorkie, Coco? And it is... until a customer at a popular patisserie drops dead face-first in a raspberry-almond tart. A competitive bakery, a newly formed friendship, and even her hotel's luxurious accommodations offer possible suspects. As Sadie sorts through a gumbo of interconnected characters, will she discover who the killer is, or will the killer discover her first?

A Flair for Truffles

Sadie Kramer's friendly offer to deliver three boxes of gourmet Valentines truffles for her neighbor's chocolate shop backfires when she arrives to find the intended recipient deceased. Even more intriguing is the fact that the elegant heart-shaped gifts were ordered by three different men. With the help of one detective and the hindrance of another, Sadie will search San Francisco for clues. But will she find out "whodunit" before the killer finds a way to stop her?

A Flair for Flip-Flops

When the body of a heartthrob celebrity washes up on the beach outside Sadie Kramer's luxury hotel suite, her fun in the sun soon turns into sleuthing with the stars. The resort's wine and appetizer gatherings, suspicious guest behavior, and casual strolls along the beach boardwalk may provide clues, but will they be enough to discover who the killer is, or will mystery and mayhem leave a Hollywood scandal unsolved?

The Moonglow Christmas Series

Mistletoe at Moonglow

The small town of Timberton, Montana, hasn't been the same since resident chef and artist, Mist, arrived, bringing a unique new age flavor to the old western town. When guests check in for the holidays, they bring along worries, fears, and broken hearts, unaware that Mist has a way of working magic in people's lives. One thing is certain: no matter how cold winter's grip is on each guest, no one leaves Timberton without a warmer heart.

Silver Bells at Moonglow

Christmas brings an eclectic gathering of visitors and locals to the Timberton Hotel each year, guaranteeing an eventful season. Add in a hint of romance, and there's more than snow in the air around the small Montana town. When the last note of Christmas carols has faded away, the soft whisper of silver bells from the front door's wreath will usher guests and townsfolk back into the world with hope for the coming year.

Gingerbread at Moonglow

The Timberton Hotel boasts an ambiance of near-magical proportions during the Christmas season. As the aromas of ginger, cinnamon, nutmeg, and molasses mix with heartfelt camaraderie and sweet romance, holiday guests share reflections on family, friendship, and life. Will decorating the outside of a gingerbread house prove easier than deciding what goes inside?

Nutcracker Sweets at Moonglow

When a nearby theatre burns down just before Christmas, cast members of *The Nutcracker* arrive at the Timberton Hotel with only a sliver of holiday joy. Camaraderie, compassion, and shared inspiration combine to help at least one hidden dream come true. As with every Christmas season, this year's guests will face the New Year with a renewed sense of hope.

Snowfall at Moonglow

As holiday guests arrive at the Timberton Hotel with hopes of a white Christmas, unseasonably warm weather hints at a less-than-wintery wonderland. But whether the snow falls or not, one thing is certain: with resident artist and chef, Mist, around, there's bound to be a little magic. No one ever leaves Timberton without renewed hope for the future.

Stand-alone: *Cranberry Bluff*

Molly Elliott's quiet life is disrupted when routine errands land her in the middle of a bank robbery. Accused and cleared of the crime, she flees both media attention and mysterious, threatening notes to run a bed and breakfast on the Northern California coast. Her new beginning is peaceful until five guests show up at the inn, each with a hidden agenda. As true motives become apparent, will Molly's past come back to haunt her, or will she finally be able to leave it behind?

For more information on Deborah Garner's books:
Facebook: https://www.facebook.com/deborahgarnerauthor
Twitter: https://twitter.com/PaigeandJake
Website: http://deborahgarner.com
Mailing list: http://bit.ly/deborahgarner